THE SCOTT AND LAURIE OKI SERIES
IN ASIAN AMERICAN STUDIES

LANGUAGE OF THE GECKOS

and other stories

GARY PAK

UNIVERSITY OF WASHINGTON PRESS

Seattle and London

This book is published with the assistance of a grant
from the Scott and Laurie Oki Endowed Fund for the
publication of Asian American Studies, established
through the generosity of Scott and Laurie Oki.

University of Washington Press
PO Box 50096, Seattle, WA 98145
www.washington.edu/uwpress

Library of Congress Cataloging-in-Publication Data
can be found at the back of this book.

The paper used in this publication is acid-free
and 90 percent recycled from at least 50 percent
post-consumer waste. It meets the minimum
requirements of American National Standard for
Information Sciences—Permanence of Paper for
Printed Library Materials, ANSI z39.48–1984. ⊗ ◉

CONTENTS

IN MEMORY OF
KENNETH CHIN MOON PAK
(1918–2004)

living with spirits,
writing as activism
A PREFACE

I

People don't believe in spirits here. . . . They live
with them.—JOHN DOMINIS HOLT, *waimea
summer*

*I hear their whispered voices from the living room. What are they
talking about? I look out through the picture window and see
the dark Koʻolau Mountains with the sun behind dying in a deep
redness. It is darkening fast outside. We have no TV set. I wish
we had one, like almost everybody else in the neighborhood.
Maybe if Daddy gets a better job.*

*I stop before entering the kitchen where Mommy and Daddy
are talking. They are talking softly, and sometimes in Korean. I
don't think they want me to hear. But I do hear. I have big ears.
I can hear the tension in their voices, especially Daddy who is
doing most of the talking. Then I poke my head in the doorway
and show myself in the light of the kitchen. I see the worried looks
on their faces. They see me and stop talking, and Mommy says,
"Gary, go back to you room. I talking to your father."*

So I go back to the darkening living room, but instead of going to my room I sit quietly on the blue couch. There's another chair in the living room and that's it. I wish we had a TV. I sit back and watch their reflection off the living room's picture window and listen to Daddy's story.

"I nevah know what to do." Daddy pauses. "I think was dah pork you gave me fo' chon-yok. Eddee, you cannot give me kwaegee kogi chonyok mogo. Cannot do that."

"But wasn't raw."

"Kwaegee is kwaegee. No argue wit' me. You know not suppose to bring pork midnight ovah dah Pali."

"Das what Ham Rodrigues tol' you?"

There is no answer from Daddy. The reflection is too blurry to see him nod, but I think that is what he does to say that Mr. Rodrigues across the street told him. Mr. Rodrigues knows a lot about Hawaiian spirits because he's one quarter Hawaiian.

"My car wen just stop," my father says. "I nevah know what fo' do. I keep on saying, 'Madame Pele, I believe in you. Madame Pele, I believe in you.'"

I cannot believe Daddy is talking like this. How can Daddy be afraid of anything? I cannot believe.

"My engine running, but dah car no move. I keep on saying, 'I believe in you, Madame Pele. I believe in you.'"

A chill enters my skinny body. I look at the Koʻolaus and now I cannot see them. They are camouflaged by the night. How fast the night has come. The chill is getting to me. I wrap my arms around my chest and look around the blackening living room. There are so many shadows in this room. There is a creak in the hallway. Is that a ghost? A cool breeze floats through the room. Chicken skin on my arms. Please don't touch me, ghost. I don't want to look into the hallway. I think about the story my father's friend, Uncle K. C., told him, about getting up in the middle of

the night and seeing a huge Hawaiian man—one ghost—filling
the doorway and Uncle leaping up and swinging his fist through
the ghost, then turning on the light and the ghost vanishing "in
thin air." I don't like going to Uncle's house, which is built near
an old Hawaiian graveyard.

I wish we had one TV to watch. Then maybe I wouldn't have
this chicken-skin feeling right now.

II

Being born and raised in Hawai'i, it is hard not to be affected
by the breathing of the land and sea. I grew up in a household
that nurtured me on Korean/Asian, Hawaiian, and American
values all at the same time. Today, the academy might say that
this is an example of the multicultural hybridity that is inher-
ent in American—perhaps, global—culture. I never saw it that
way, and even now it is hard for me to define the way I was
brought up if I'm to describe it in contemporary academic
terms; it would sound as if my life was culturally compart-
mentalized, divided into disparate, perhaps disruptive, fac-
tions. Better simply stated, my culture is what it is, a product
of the many crisscrossings of various cultures in Hawai'i, a
working out of the differences and similarities between the
indigenous culture and the many others that invaded or were
introduced here. Local people[1] are aware of these influences
and, for the most part, play with them in linguistic strides and

1. By this, I mean people who live in this hybridized culture of Hawai'i
that includes its unique language (i.e., Pidgin English), foods, habits, etc.
The term "local" is not necessarily a term of race, though many locals may
see it as such. See Stephen Sumida's preface in *And the View from the Shore:*
Literary Traditions of Hawai'i (Seattle: University of Washington Press, 1991)
for a reasonable introduction to this term.

banter (e.g., "I get Japanese-Chinese-Filipino-Hawaiian blood"; or, "Must be dah Pākē/Korean/Filipino/etc. [choose one] in me das making me act dis way").

On the other hand, it is inaccurate to say that there isn't any tension in this melding. My life, at various junctures and times, has been one of "grudging acceptance"[2] of this mixing. Contradictions due to cultural differences do arise and sometimes intensify, though they oftentimes lead to resolution. When I studied the revisionist histories of Korea/Asia/Hawai'i/Polynesia and became more aware of the suffering, the humiliation, the genocide, the outright warmongering criminal acts, etc., that British, Japanese, American, etc.—choose one according to the historical context—imperialism had committed against the peoples of the world, I then began to understand the nature of these contradictions. For example, as a ninth grader during the height of the Vietnam War, I was an unabashed supporter of an American foreign policy that championed itself as the defender of "democracy" and as the God-given deterrent to the spread of godless communism, but it shook me when I finally started to understand that U.S. "democracy" was built on deception and nourished by plundering the peoples of the world. I came to see that the Vietnam War was a war of liberation against American imperialism, a war that was formerly a struggle of the Vietnamese people against French colonialism. I came to see that the annexation of Hawai'i into the American sphere, which subsequently led to statehood in 1959, was rather an illegal overthrow of the Hawaiian nation and the subjugation of a proud people, a part of the United State's incipient plan of world domination. I came to see that the bombing of Hiroshima and

2. To paraphrase local Chinese-American poet Wing Tek Lum.

Nagasaki (after the U.S. bloc had already decidedly leveled the Japanese imperialists to their knees), the massacres in No Gun Ri and My Lai, and more recently what is happening in Iraq as manifestations stemming from a thoroughly racist policy against nonwhite people, something that had been also part and parcel of its domestic practice against its own people, such as the genocidal attacks on Native Americans, the brutal enslavement of African Americans, and the suppression of the American working class in the nineteenth and early twentieth centuries. These altogether were and are attacks on the people of the world because of class, race, gender, and religion.

It was very hard to realize that one part of myself was the reason for the destruction of the other(s). But it was a contradiction that I swore to approach head on and resolve.

III

In a quiet moment of the first day that we bring home our first child from the hospital, I get to watch mother and baby when they sleep. I look at the pureness on both of their faces, both exhausted by this entire taxing ordeal. I watch baby's face, eyes closed serenely in sleep, lips sculpted so perfectly. I think about him, about his future. What will he be? What will he do in life? What will he become?

In our son I find my calling.

IV

Imperialism . . . is an act of geographical violence, through which virtually every space in the world is explored, charted, and finally brought

> under control. For the native, the history of colo-
> nial servitude is inaugurated by loss of the local-
> ity to the outsider; its geographical identity must
> thereafter be searched for and somehow restored.
> Because of the presence of the colonizing outsider,
> the land is recoverable at first only through the
> imagination.—EDWARD W. SAID, *Culture and
> Imperialism*

I don't want our son to feel discriminated in this society that is said to be ours but really isn't. I want him to have a fair shake in life's opportunities. I am acutely aware of the inequities that our son will have to face, that he already faces from the day of his birth because of his living in a society based on approved distinctions of race, class, and gender. A society that is bent on oppressing masses of people for the betterment of a few *trés riches* families. A society that tries to brainwash every citizen to think that the ruling order is justified because those in power have worked hard and are innately smarter, nay superior, than the rest of us dumb masses, and thus it is God-given that they rule over all of us. A society that promotes a rigid code of aesthetics based on race, class, and gender, and if you don't fit in, then tough luck.

No, I don't want our son to be already handicapped in a society that has pegged him in a category because of his ethnicity, gender, class, the lack of money that his parents have, the place where he is born, etc. I will fight against a system that wants him to be its slave, a system that is going to tell him that he is already inferior to the sons and daughters of the so-called powerful. No, this will never happen to him. Never. We don't have a silver spoon to put in his mouth—my wife and

I would never think of doing so anyway even if we had the opportunity, with our kind of consciousness. If there is anything that we can give him (and other siblings that he may have later), it is the gift of being able to think critically and independently. And to be able to express himself bravely.

There are so many positive stories to be told about life in Hawai'i, so many stories and traditions of Hawai'i that are not being recorded. Now I am determined to write stories that will not only reach out to my son but also to create stories that will be part of a culture that he can claim as rightfully his, something that no one can take away from him, that no one can usurp from him and thus deny his existence to *be*, to *be proud*, to *be his own*.

So I begin writing my stories. Stories that he can call his own. Stories that his future siblings and hopefully his friends can call theirs. If I don't do this, I will be haunted if he ever becomes brainwashed by the American mainstream, by the eurocentric media crap that would make him feel inferior when he shouldn't. I want him to be given the opportunity to grow intellectually, physically, culturally, sexually, socially, and, perhaps most importantly, spiritually, as much as possible on his *own* terms.

V

I write in my notebook during the breaks in my cab between taking fares. I sketch caricatures of some of my riders, turning them into characters that perhaps may find their way into one of my stories. I write during the breaks while taking local people to the nightclubs, sailors to Hotel Street and Waikīkī, the prostitutes to their appointments, the drug addicts to their fixes. I write in the time before, between, and after the two times I get robbed. I am writing my impressions of life, my visions of what I feel should be. My commitment to writing as activism becomes unshakeable.

VI

> I took the energy it takes to pout and wrote some blues.—DUKE ELLINGTON

I offer *Language of the Geckos and Other Stories* as a look into a world that I don't know completely but one in which I live and am learning more and more about every day. I offer these stories as interpretations of my continuing activism and commitment to "this earth of humankind," to paraphrase the title of the remarkable novel by Indonesian writer Pramoedya Ananta Toer, with the hope that they may help to make this a better, more humanistic world.

LANGUAGE OF THE GECKOS

and other stories

A HOUSE OF MIRRORS

Miss Doris Takeshita, retired elementary school principal, lived in a large three-story house at the corner of what was once two intersecting streets, what was now a dead end, with the construction of a freeway that had plowed through the old neighborhood. She lived in the house that was built by her father, who had the distinction of being the first American-educated dentist of Japanese extraction to open a private practice in Honolulu, in the then-Territory of Hawaii.

Dr. Takeshita, deceased after forty-nine years of successful practice, learned the art of teeth cleaning and drilling and the like from a well-respected school of dentistry in Boston. Though he seldom left that small rented room in the black ghetto where his school was marginally situated, on Sundays, when the weather was nice, he'd take a break from his demanding studies and take the train to the end of the Green Line, getting off in the white suburbs. He'd spend entire mornings walking in the parks and along the streets, admiring the beautifully constructed homes with their tall sloping roofs and large viewing windows. One morning a houseowner, Professor Percival R. Wilcox, befriended him and invited him in for lemonade, and the future Dr. Takeshita accepted with much gratefulness. Professor Wilcox, of Boston College, almost correctly identified him as a medical student at Harvard, erring slightly on both counts. The young student now saw with bright, widened eyes what it was like inside one of the houses which he admired so much. And, in time, after establishing himself in a steadily growing practice in downtown Honolulu, he, too, lived in a house like Professor Wilcox's. Dr. Takeshita purchased a sizable lot in lower Makīkī and hired a contractor to build expressly the house he had seen in Chestnut Hill; and though he had neither photo nor sketch of that particular house, the finished product was a remarkable facsimile, remarkable in the sense that every detail was realized from the picture in Dr. Takeshita's memory.

The house was constructed years before Doris Takeshita was born; it would be a good decade before Dr. Takeshita would marry his nurse. But Doris grew up securely in this grand house, which contrasted greatly in size and style from the other tract homes of the neighborhood and was the object of envy for even some of the wealthy haole families living in Nuʻuanu and Mānoa valleys. There was a large attic that became very warm when the weather was hot, and a dark musty cellar that remained cool even in those hot times, both being, however, unconventional for homes in Hawaiʻi. And there was a large library, which the doctor never used, that was Doris's favorite room. Doris never knew another house for her entire life.

Doris's mother died of tuberculosis when Doris was first beginning to form sentences in her speech; though there was a housekeeper who thereafter looked after her, for the most part Doris was left to fend for herself in this large, airy house. To brighten things up, her father had the exterior of the house painted from its chestnut brown to an oyster white; and to further enhance the mood, he had Doris's mother's invaluable collection of Japanese woodblock prints taken down from the walls of the living room and main hall, and directed the mountings of large mirrors in their place.

Doris liked the mirrors. During the afternoons after school, when the housekeeper would be preparing dinner, she'd sit in the living room with one of her favorite books from the home library and ever so often deliberately raise her eyes from the text, looking at herself in one of the mirrors with a promise and anticipation that perhaps she might find the story's heroine looking back at her instead of seeing her own dark eyes. But no: her hair was not blond and braided; her eyes were not a pale blue like a weak morning sky. The bright red calico dress Doris wore almost habitually was the closest representation to the heroine of the book.

Sometimes on Saturday mornings when Mr. Johiro the gardener came to tend the yard, Doris would sit with an open book next to a sunny living room window and watch the yardman work. She liked the smell of freshly turned earth or cut grass, and sometimes a half hour would pass before she'd realize that she had not turned a page. The Saturday mornings at the window were quiet and enjoyable until Mr. Johiro began bringing his son, who was about the same age as Doris. On his first Saturday at the Takeshitas', the boy startled Doris by sneaking up to the open window, its screen taken down for cleaning, and throwing a rosebud at her. Doris retreated from the window and from that time on cloistered herself in the library or in her own room until the gardener and his son left in their rickety, avocado-colored Ford pickup.

But at least once during a Saturday morning, she'd secretly look down from the window of her bedroom on the second floor and try to catch a glimpse of the boy. Sometimes she'd see both father and son backbent, weeding the flower beds below her; sometimes she'd see the boy climbing one of the many trees in the yard; sometimes she couldn't see them, they'd be on the other side of the house, so she'd go to the bathroom that was across the hall and stand on a stool and look down into the rose bushes to see if she could spot them.

Once, while weeding the flower beds, Mr. Johiro looked up at the sky, wiping the perspiration from his forehead, and happened to see Doris watching them. He doffed his wide-rim papale and waved it with a smile. Quickly, she darted from the window and threw herself on her bed, burying her face in a pillow and closing her eyes tightly to wish away the embarrassment. Then, returning to her chair, she opened her book and read each word aloud. But she could not concentrate on the meaning of words and pictures, for all she could think about was the embarrassment of being caught watching them. Later that afternoon, after Mr. Johiro and son had left, she returned to the living room window with the intention to read, but all she could see in her mind was the boy running and jumping in the yard and climbing the trees, and all she could smell was the scent of the boy's rose.

In the afternoons, if it was nice out, the housekeeper would take Doris for a walk to the nearby park. Sometimes they'd sit and watch the neighborhood boys play baseball, and sometimes Mrs. Iwabashi would tell stories about her children—she had five girls and three boys. Sometimes she'd tell Doris Japanese folktales.

One night when Doris was in bed, talking quietly to a

favorite stuffed doll, Lucy, she heard a voice calling her name. It was a soothing voice, a voice as warm and comfortable as a calm heartbeat. At first she thought it was Lucy talking to her, for Lucy often did talk to her, though not in the voice she was now hearing. So she questioned Lucy, but Lucy was silent. And she asked Lucy again if it was she who was speaking, and again Lucy did not make a sound. Doris softly stroked Lucy's long red braids and told her that it was all right if she wanted to remain silent, that she would not be angry at Lucy if that was her choice. But the voice again called Doris, and she realized that the voice was not Lucy's but was coming from somewhere else in the room. She wasn't startled, for she had often heard voices in the house talking to themselves, though this time was the first that a particular voice chose to address her.

Doris listened for a while to the melodious rendering of her name. Then, after the fifth or sixth calling, she answered.

"Pretend you are one of us," the voice returned.

"What do you want me to pretend?" Doris asked.

"You can be Alice or Heidi or Nancy or whomever you want. Then you can be happy."

"But I am happy."

"Or, if you wish, you can pretend to be their playmate. They've always wanted to play with you."

Doris smiled at the suggestion. But she became confused.

"How can I be like them?" she asked. "I don't know how to do this."

"Just look in one of the mirrors downstairs," the voice said, "and close your eyes and dream of your favorite playmate. You'll find yourself playing with her or turning into her before you know it."

For an hour or so, a restless Doris thought about this but didn't dare go downstairs by herself in the dark. Finally she fell asleep, and when she awoke the next morning, she had forgotten what the voice had told her.

That afternoon, however, as she sat on the couch in the living room and stared into one of the room's large mirrors, she remembered what the voice had told her and began to follow its instructions, an excitement enlarging her eyes. But nothing happened; all she saw was her black hair and her brown squinting eyes and a blemishless complexion that was still darker than the one she wished for. She repeated herself, closing her eyes and making another wish, and when she reopened them, she was again disappointed. It was frustrating. She lay her head on a soft cushion and cried, and she lay there for a long while, gradually nodding off to a nap and dreaming about absolutely nothing at all.

She was wakened by a tiny voice, her eyes fluttering open as her ears sought the source of the calling. Thinking it was the little boy playing a trick on her, she realized that it was a Monday and not a Saturday. She sat up, rubbed her eyes, and looked across the room to the wall where another large mirror was mounted. In a lower corner of the mirror, a little girl with braided, straw-colored hair and a freckled nose was smiling at her.

"Who are you?" Doris asked.

"I am you," the girl said. Then she disappeared into the edge of the mirror.

Doris's heart bound with excitement. Anxiously, she crawled to the mirror, hesitated under the bottom edge, then, closing her eyes, counted to five and stood up.

A broad landscape of apple trees and green rounded hills unfolded before her. A country road began from the lower left corner of the mirror nearest to her and zigzagged diagonally to the upper right. Doris heard giggles. The little girl, holding a hand over her mouth, was half hidden behind a tree.

A long moment passed before Doris realized that it was she herself who was giggling.

Now in the afternoons after coming home from school, the mirrors of the house became her playground. In those magical afternoons, Doris could be any of her book friends. She would be Alice or Nancy or whoever. In that giant living room of mirrors, she'd swirl her arms and play out plots and wear the oversized, mothballed clothing and jewelry of her mother, and she'd pretend to be that perfectly beautiful princess—long blonde braids, Rapunzelesque—waiting for that gallant handsome prince—brave prince, brave man— of her life and dreams. The mirrors were the homes of her dearest wishes. And for the rest of her younger years, the mirrors provided her with hours of unsurpassable entertainment. But, like any childhood, the fun and fantasy of childhood was later outgrown.

She was educated at the local university to be near her father. And she never married, though there was a young man she met in her sophomore year in college whom she liked somewhat, and she went out with him several times to the movies. But nothing really came of their relationship, at least nothing was initiated on Doris's part. She desired something more in a someone that this young man did not— could not—possess. Her kind of someone was dashing and bold and perhaps adorned with a thin moustache and a noble smile and dark curls for hair. And when the lights came on after the end of a movie, she'd look at Peter, and though his face was quite handsome in a boyish kind of way, it was not the kind of handsomeness that she thought was handsome. Then the war broke out, and Peter enlisted and was ordered to the European front. Before leaving, he proposed to Doris, and she uncomfortably yet unhesitatingly refused. He became a member of the heroic 442nd and was one of those lucky ones who survived. The second day back home, dressed in his pressed uniform and with two medals to support his talk of an honorable discharge, Peter went to court her. But he found that she was seeing someone else, a haole serviceman stationed at Fort Shafter. (She never introduced Harry from Pennsylvania to her father since she knew that her father would have had a fit. She often met Harry downtown in the front of Hawaii Theatre. They'd pretend not to know each other, but the minute they were in the dimly lit lobby, they'd hold each other's hands and sit in the back row. When the darkness of the theatre cloaked them, they'd brave whatever kind of romance that her fancy permitted them to have.) Young Peter was crushed when he heard the name of that someone else sighed at him, but being a good sport, he said goodbye, his eyes now heavy, and wished her the best. With hands in pockets and head bent, he shuffled out the house and down the twilit sidewalk and headed to a mainland law school, where he graduated in the middle of his class after three long years (and later became a powerful Honolulu attorney). Then Harry left suddenly, without a word, and Doris was devastated, refusing to leave the house for an entire year, during which time she never spent more than a few seconds to view her deflated self in any of the house's many mirrors.

Thinking that it was Peter who had broken his daughter's heart, a saddened Dr. Takeshita tried to offset his daughter's despondency by making a habitual visit to a downtown bookseller at the beginning of every week to purchase an armload of popular novels for the pleasure of his grieving daughter. After this long period nursing her bruised ego, she finally got a job using her education degree. She became a teacher with the state system, went back to school during the summers, took a year's sabbatical to earn a master's degree, and rose surely to become the principal of Kānewai Elementary School. And she was never married, except to her job.

Dr. Takeshita died when Doris was in her late forties, leaving her as the sole beneficiary of his entire estate, which was relatively considerable. The continuation of Doris's comfortable lifestyle was guaranteed for as long as she lived. That was a certainty.

The technology of the nineteen-seventies reached Doris in the eighties. (She had already retired from the Department of Education for a year and was drawing a nice compensation, though she hardly needed it.) Persuaded by advertisements on the television and in magazines and newspapers, and influenced by the loneliness that was a direct result of Dr. Takeshita's death (she had very few friends, who called on her infrequently), Doris finally convinced herself of a consumer need that she never knew she had. One day, she walked to the nearest appliance store and bought a videocassette recorder, a very fine one, the most expensive and most sophisticated that the store had to offer. (Doris was a pushover when it came to salesmen and their slick presentations; and, of course, money was not a question.) Along with the machine, she purchased a boxful of classic video movies. Now, in the convenience of her home, Doris could view the repeat performances of Clark Gable, Vivian Leigh, Rita Hayworth, Spencer Tracy, Cary

Grant, Jean Arthur, Rock Hudson, Marilyn Monroe, Doris Day
and so on and on, all the stars of the yesteryears who were close
to her yesteryear heart.

While watching Hitchcock's *Vertigo* late one night, she heard
a voice calling. At first startled, wondering suddenly if the
housekeeper had forgotten to lock the back kitchen door, she
surprised herself by associating the voice with the one from
her childhood, a time she had not thought about for many
years. Raising her eyes to the mirror that was mounted behind
the television, her heart thumping in a bewildering pattern,
she held her breath, not knowing what she might see. Though
she remembered vaguely its representation in the mirror—it
had been so many years ago, fifty-two to be exact, since she
was introduced to her other self, that other self that had given
her hours of dreamy joy—she had forgotten how this had
entertained her. Now she could feel only a horror that someone or something gruesome, perhaps dangerous, might be staring back at her. She passed her hand from her breast to her
mouth, then centered it over her heart, readying herself for a
jolt. What she did see startled her terribly.

For a long moment she stared at the image of Kim Novak.
Doris glanced at the television screen and saw James Stewart
as a private investigator trailing Miss Novak, who was acting
as the supposedly unfaithful wife of his client. Now Doris
looked back at the mirror and discovered that the actress was
wearing Doris's very own faded nightgown, the one she had
on right now—and how beautiful she looked in it! Looking
away, she regarded her arms, her hands, and they were covered with the same old skin patched with ugly liver spots. But
there, in the mirror, she was beautiful, blonde, cool, confident,
a sex goddess supreme of Hollywood. It was . . . so marvelous.

Doris regarded the television. There was James Stewart persuading Miss Novak to change her makeup. When she looked back at the mirror, there she was again: the Queen of the Screen.

The transformation was wonderful, absolutely tremendously wonderful. She winked naughtily into the mirror, then got off the couch and began dancing all over the living room in luxurious circles like a dervish. She took the cover off the couch and draped it over her shoulders, and it became a cape of red velvet and white satin. And she was now Helen of Troy, and great brave men would fight over her, they'd launch a thousand ships just on the account of her beautiful face.

She woke up the next morning with her usual equilibrium upended. Did she imagine all of that last night? Was it a dream? Or was it real? Rising slowly from the bed, she looked in the mirror of her bureau and saw herself as she expected: an old, tired-looking woman with bags under her eyes; face and arms dappled with old-age spots; skin the color of ash; and locks of dyed-hair suspended stiffly, defying the laws of gravity. It was a reflection that she wished wasn't there. She would rather see a young and beautiful Kim Novak, or anything else besides that worn and wrinkled Oriental face that she seldom looked at for longer than a few touch-up moments.

Washing and then dressing herself in a comfortable shift, she went downstairs to the living room. The television was still on. She chided herself for being forgetful. But where was the housekeeper anyway? The housekeeper should have turned it off. But had Doris really become Kim Novak last night? She ejected the cassette from the VCR, glancing at the title. Yes, she had watched that movie. Was it possible that she had become what she thought she had become?

This is all nonsense, she reminded herself. A child can pre-

tend, not an adult. Why am I talking this way? A never-never
land! Only child's play.

But the alluring possibility of this child's world became an
obsession with her. Though repeatedly warning herself against
thinking such thoughts, at the same time she could not help
but think that the impossible was possible. The belief grew
stronger with the length of the day, and though she opposed
it with token defense, the battle was decided. By day's end, when
the housekeeper had left, a strange thing happened. She looked
into one mirror and saw a mixing of grays and blacks and
browns and pinks, and the colors swirled as if they were inert
paints on an artist's palette blending into two-dimensional life.
She closed her eyes and a silvery screen manifested. And when
she finally opened her eyes, she became, once again, Kim Novak.

And this went on, night after night, her becoming a screen
goddess of her picking: one night, a Doris Day; another night,
a Jean Arthur; another, a Greta Garbo; another, a Rosalind
Russell. She was not Doris Takeshita anymore: retiree, spin-
ster, aging last member of the Takeshita clan. It was good to
feel that way. In the quiet of night, all it took to make that
narcotic-like metamorphosis was slipping a video cassette into
the tape player. A minute into the movie and she'd be her other
self, reciting lines by heart, those strings of rapturous words
that brought romance into her bosom. Before the end of each
tape, she'd be waltzing up the stairs of an old mansion to her
room where waited the gray-cloaked man of the night. (Yes,
her VCR came equipped with an automatic shut-off feature,
the function of which she now mastered, and a recently purchased timer turned off the television at exactly two A.M.)

Early one afternoon, while cleaning her desk, the maid
informed her that a visitor had come. Asking who it was, Doris

was told that the visitor had mentioned that he was an old family friend. She went downstairs and found an unfamiliar, sixtyish man waiting in the living room.

"Yes? Can I help you?"

"Excuse me, but are you Dr. Takeshita's daughter?" the man asked politely, smiling.

"Yes. What do you want?"

"I dunno if you remembah me, but . . . " The man glanced shyly across the room, rubbing his chin. "My name is Sunao Johiro. My fathah used to be yo' fathah's gardenah."

Doris pondered this for a moment, then an ambivalent smile came to her face. "Yes, I remember your father. And you used to come with him on Saturdays, isn't that right?"

The yardman's son nodded at the recognition, a deferent smile flourishing on his face.

"So how have you been?" she asked. "Can I get you something to drink? Some coffee?"

"I no want to impose. Actually, I was jus' passing by. I live in Ka'imukī now. I jus' was passing by when I noticed da house and I started remembering all da good times I use to have here when I use to come wit' my fathah. My fathah use to like taking care Dr. Takeshita's yard. So I thought I come drop by, jus' fo' say hello."

"Oh, it's very nice of you to drop by. Shelley? Can you get us some coffee? Please sit down, Sunao. It's Sunao, right?"

"Yes. Thank you."

"So how is your father?"

"My fathah's okay. He retired long time already. Eighty-nine years old come next month."

"My, he's living a nice long life."

Sunao nodded, pursing his lips.

"My father died twelve years ago," she said.

"Yes. I sorry about his passing. I read his obituary in da newspepah. I took my fathah to his funeral."

"Oh. Thank you." Doris tried to remember their faces—Sunao's face—at the funeral, but she couldn't. "And so . . . what have you been doing with yourself lately?"

"I retired three years ago. I was working fo' da City and County."

"Oh, as a what? I retired from the State a little over a year ago. I was an administrator with the Department of Education." The coffee was served; Doris stirred in some cream and sugar. "How do you like your coffee, Sunao?"

"I like mine black, if is okay."

"So what did you do at the City and County?"

"I was one gardenah. Like my fathah. I use to work at da Rose Garden right next to da zoo." He sipped his coffee.

"Yes, I know that place. There are some very nice flowers there. I went there a few times, but I don't remember seeing you there."

"Yes, it was a very nice place to work. We try make dat place nice so people can enjoy. Is a good feeling to see all dose buds blooming all ovah da place. Everybody used to come and look and touch and smell all dose flowers. Was most beautiful in da morning. Das when all da dew is all ovah da branches and leaves and da flowers."

"It must have been beautiful . . . working there."

"Yes," he said. He sipped his coffee. "It is very beautiful. Very, very beautiful."

Sunao's visit was an enjoyable surprise for Doris. At the end of the visit, she gave him an open invitation to the house.

Sitting in the old library armchair and gazing across the room to the window brightened by the afternoon sun, she remembered the man as a young boy: puttering among the flower beds and rose bushes with his squatting father; climbing the big mango tree in the back; running circles around his father pushing the lawnmower. Then she remembered the rosebud that the boy had tossed at her, which she had taken from under the living room couch where she had kicked it that night when her father was asleep, snoring softly on the very armchair she was now sitting on (though, at that time, it was situated in the living room in front of the radio set). She had put the rose with the rest of her childhood valuables in a small vanity box made of sandalwood.

She desired to find that box, to touch that rose that the boy had given her those many years ago. She knew that the box was somewhere in the house; she never threw old things away. Was it in the attic? Was it in the hall closet that was stuffed full with her father's clothes and papers?

The attic was hot, making her perspire freely. She had not gone into it for years. After one search through a labyrinth of old suitcases and furniture and whatnot, she found the dusty box in a far corner, sitting squarely on top of a stack of old *Life* magazines. She unlatched the cover—is the rose in here? did I throw it away years ago? has it disintegrated?—then decided not to open it in the attic but in the library. Clasping the box, she went to the second floor where the air was cooler and less oppressive. In the hallway mirror, she saw a film of cobwebs and dust on her hair and face. Setting the box on a small hall table, she went to the bathroom and washed herself under a steaming shower, scrubbing her skin clean of the dirt.

Refreshed, she opened the box in the library next to the window. Under yellowed newspaper clippings, old letters and tarnished costume jewelry, she found the rose, dried and brittle, the color of oxblood. The flower was in good condition, with two petals broken off. Carefully, she lifted the flower from the box by its stem, then cradled it in the palm of her hand. A serene feeling came to her. A short while later, with her eyes growing heavy, she fell into a deep sleep.

That night she could not sleep, so she watched a televised Cagney movie. Despite the commercial interruptions, the characters of the movie again came alive in the mirrors. But this time she was annoyed. Doris turned the set off, and the voice followed Doris up to the bedroom, where it scolded, cried, and finally threathened Doris, demanding her to turn the set back on. But Doris refused. Loud laughter began to reverberate off the walls. Doris clamped her hands over her ears and curled herself into a ball. She cried for help, but the voice drowned her appeal. Finally, the laughter moved away, diminishing down the hall and stairs.

Sunao's face came to Doris, and she felt a promise of hope. Perhaps he could help her. Perhaps he would be able to save her from the madness in the house.

The following day she waited for Sunao. Was her invitation insincere? Perhaps she had been too aggressive in offering an invitation. Perhaps she should have been more persuasive. It wasn't her fault that Sunao was unattractive, that his complexion was dark and oily, and that he was thin and had a lot of white hairs.

But more than anything else, she wished he was here. She ordered the housekeeper to roast a large chicken, just in case he might be there for dinner. But he never came.

That night, the voices of the house came out of the walls and glamorous movie stars showed themselves in the mirrors. Doris left the lights on throughout the house. She retreated to her bedroom and took refuge under the covers, even though the night was warm and windless and the termites were out circling beneath the dull porch light. For the first time in her life she wished she could leave the house. It was a hard thing to do, but perhaps Sunao was her Knight-in-Shining-Armor and he'd whisk her away from this nightmare. Perhaps he'd rescue her from this house of madness, this house of mirrors, to live out their lives somewhere faraway and pleasant. Like how it was in the movies.

The next morning she scanned the listings in the phone book, but could not find an entry for Sunao Johiro. Does he have a phone? She watched from her bedroom window the children playing down the street in the park. Then she imagined Sunao as a small boy again, romping on the wide lawn, the yard which she never really knew. Maybe she ought to get out of the house and work in the yard, she thought. Maybe it would be good to get her hands dirty.

It was a convincing thought for her.

Donning some old clothes, she went out to the garage where the rusty garden tools of her father were stored. (The present Filipino yardman always brought his own.) She weeded a small section of the flower bed beneath the living room window and then called it quits at about half past noon. The heat was getting to her and she was hungry, but it felt good to work in the garden, to get her hands dirty and the perspiration flowing so freely. It felt very good. She looked at the back door and listened to the sounds of Shelley cleaning the kitchen, thinking how the housekeeper must think how crazy she was to work in the yard after all of these years.

Doris leaned back against the wall of the house under the shade of a lemon tree and laughed. She looked up at the bright sun that sparkled through the leaves and thought of the joy that Sunao must have felt when he was a small boy working the yard with his father. She wished that she had not been so shy in her younger years. Wouldn't it have been wonderful if she had experienced the joys of youth with Sunao, running and tumbling in the rose garden, climbing the trees in her father's large yard? She thought of the dried rose in her box and wanted so much to hold it right then. Looking at the sun for the length of a deep, cleansing breath, she entered the house and took a long hot shower.

In the library, Doris opened the box and gently placed the rose on her lap. Another petal had broken off. The new air seemed to be more damaging than rejuvenating for the dead flower. She picked up the petal and crushed it with her fingertips, sprinkling the fine dust over the rest of the contents.

The housekeeper came into the library and announced that lunch was ready. She left the room, but a moment later returned.

"Oh, Miss Takeshita? You had a call when you were out in the yard. It was from Mr. Johiro."

"Mr. Johiro? Why didn't you call me in?"

"He didn't want me to bother you. He asked me if you were busy and I said that you were working in the—"

"How stupid can you be! You should have called me!"

"I'm sorry, Miss Takeshita."

"You're sorry! How can you be so stupid?"

"I'm sorry."

"Did he leave his number?"

"No. He said he would call back."

"Stupid! Must I teach you how to answer a phone? You must always—ALWAYS—ask for a number. Stupid! Stupid! Stupid!"

"I'm sorry."

"Go! Get back to your work."

Biting her upper lip to keep her composure, Shelley left the room.

An angry fire, fueled by the stupidity of the housekeeper, burned in Doris. Then she noticed that in her rage she had inadvertently crushed most of the flower. The shock was just too much for her. She returned what was left of the rose to the box. Folding her arms over her chest and rocking herself in the chair, she burst into tears. "How stupid! Stupid! Stupid!"

Sunao Johiro did not call back that afternoon, or the days following, those days of anguish and waiting for Doris. She never went out of the house again and was always a ring away from the phone. And everything seemed to upset her. She scolded the maid for being one minute too long on the phone. She complained that the cushions on the sofa were not in their right positions. She cursed when the meat was too rare or too well done. And so on. She also ordered the housekeeper to bring her meals in the living room so that she'd be close to the telephone. She even began sleeping there.

But it was terrible tradeoff; for when night came, the mirrors in the living room came alive. Though she wanted to run to her bedroom or out of the house, she reasoned it to be more important to wait for Sunao's call. The voices of the house taunted her, even haunted her in her dreams. All along, she held on to the hope that Sunao would give her that call or just drop by.

But the man who was supposed to save her, who was supposed to be her Knight-in-Shining-Armor, never called and never returned for a visit. And with Shelley's quitting, Doris Takeshita once and for all closed the windows and doors of the house from the outside world.

The only person to have any kind of contact with her was the Filipino gardener, who worked on the yard twice a month. He'd only see her thin, procelain-like white hand through the narrow crack of the opened door when he'd ask politely for the money she owed him for the month's yard maintenance and for reimbursement of the groceries he'd buy for her, which he'd leave on the back porch. She always gave him a generous tip and the grocery list for the next time, though never uttering a word. And he never saw her take in the groceries; she'd wait for the yardman to leave and for the cover of darkness.

The voices of the house became less mischievous with her. They became generous with new affection, as if realizing now that their status in the house was forever and ever, Amen. Doris's heroines sighed with a pleasant relief for a last time. At least now they were guaranteed to live out their lives, Amen.

And one night Doris was Betty Grable strutting around in those classic legs. And another night she was Grace Kelly being swooned by the husky voice of her leading man. And another night she was Ingrid Bergman. And she danced and lived the life of romance and climbed tall hills and mountains and flew on aeroplanes and trampled through wild exotic jungles and, and . . .

LANGUAGE OF THE GECKOS

The geckos were all over Gabriel Hoʻokano's house, but the situation never bothered him for the simple reason that they had always been there. Generations and generations of geckos had populated the Hoʻokano property, even before the house (which Gabriel had built himself) existed. Gabriel knew the genealogy of the geckos, or the moʻo as he would correctly call them, since he regarded their lineage and his to be one and the same. He would call a particular gecko Uncle or Auntie; and with the death of his wayward brother Jacob, the kahuna of Waiola Valley, the newest gecko to appear on Gabriel's nightly screen was given the name Kopa, Jacob's childhood nickname.

It was amazing that even with a failing memory Gabriel never forgot any of the names of the hundreds—perhaps thousands—of geckos that surrounded him. What was even more astonishing was his ability to communicate—rather, "talk story"—with the moʻo, with the exception of the new one, Kopa, who had never once kah-kah-kahed since his advent at the Hoʻokano house (though he had taken a royal share of termites, flies, mosquitoes and other resident arthropods).

Even if Kopa never talked to him, Gabriel made it a habit to talk with him anyway, for he knew Kopa was hiding in some nook of the porch and listening. In the early evenings, after finishing the supper that he now often cooked, Gabriel would talk stories to Kopa while his common-law wife, Mary, and his first cousin Harriet were washing the dishes and talking stories. (Harriet had taken the habit, as requested adamantly by Mary and accepted by a not-so-enthusiastic Gabriel, of having her meals at the Hoʻokano residence; for the most part, she had moved in, taking quarters in the back bedroom of the house, which was ideal for her since from the window she had a near-panoramic sweep of her pasture, which bordered the back of Gabriel's property. An old, rickety, termite-ravished, one-car garage partly blocked her view of the right side of her lot, but it was a one-minute stroll to her beloved cows.) Gabriel would relate the day's events to Kopa, and if he could not remember what had happened, he would make them up. This was done with an understanding of his brother's situation: Kopa, frolicking in the spiritual world that made him know about almost everything, would know how to interpret Gabriel's stories and turn them into truths.

Gabriel noticed how boisterous the geckos had become over the past few days (with the exception of Kopa, though Gabriel did note how he had become a bit edgy at times, skittering back and forth across the dusty screen faster than usual, as if anticipating a big storm), with the geckos on the mauka side of the house being contentious with the geckos of the front porch. They'd meet at the intersecting corner of the house, usually near the eaves, and have it out. Most of the time

Gabriel heard them argue about how much more termites the other side was getting, though once there was a savage fight that involved two geckos locked in each other's jaws. Gabriel, who couldn't stand the sight of a family fighting (there had just been too much of that in his immediate, human family), shooed them off with a bulldog look and a loud *kah-kaht!* But the next evening Gabriel heard more racket, this time coming from the makai Diamond Head corner of the house. And this continued for the next three days. (Or was it four?) Something was definitely bugging the moʻo, and Gabriel found no rest when the moʻo were in such a troubled state.

And then it rained hard for five days and nights, which gave some peace to the residents of the house. The heavy wet air seemed to pacify the geckos and, correspondingly, Gabriel too. The rain had come in from the ocean, and at first the showers were intermittent. When there was a break in the rain, Gabriel would look towards Waiola Valley (where his brother had lived), which was lost in low-lying clouds. "Kopa, I know you behind all of dis," Gabriel would say deliberately and repeatedly in the day, but with a smile, since Gabriel knew that Jacob, even after years and years of indifference and downright mistrust, really had a soft spot in his soul. Once, after gazing towards the rainy clouds by Waiola and making his comment, Gabriel was sure that he heard a subdued kah-kahing somewhere above him.

But on the second day, the rains came down hard, and they got harder as the day progressed. By the third day, a small lake began forming in the front yard of the Hoʻokano house. Gabriel called John Kim, the newspaper district manager, to temporarily terminate delivery of the morning daily. Now Gabriel would look up at the always cloudy sky and the rain and begin cursing his brother: "And den! You going float my house away or what?!"

Strange things began to float in the growing lake. At first, Gabriel took no notice until Mary peeled off a scrap of newspaper that had washed up on the second-from-the-bottom porch step.

"Look, Gabe, how old dis newspaper is."

Gabriel continued rocking in his chair, wrapped in that moldy mood of his that was getting moldier by the moment.

"August 19, 1956," Mary announced, as if the date had a special significance.

It didn't, but the uttered month and last digit echoed through those mossy arches in Gabriel's mind. Funny that with all his forgetfulness he was able to remember the exact date of his induction into the United States armed services: August 6, 1944.

"Mo' bettah I should have quit when I was ahead," he said.

"What was dat?" inquired a half-listening Harriet, who was sitting on the other end of the patio.

Turning to his cousin, Gabriel repeated his comment and added, "Das what history is all about, I think, about having to do things not yo' own way but den you da one gotta face da truth or consequences."

And funny how Gabriel's words triggered a recurrence of a bitter memory in Harriet, of the day when she received the telegram declaring her husband's death on the U.S.S. *Indianapolis*, one week after its sinking. Harriet didn't cry, but she had a sudden desire to visit her cows.

"I'm going," she said to no one and everyone.

"Where you going?" Mary asked with alarm, looking up from her self-appointed work of piecing together the soggy bits of the old newspaper. "How you going out of dis house wit' all of dis rain . . . and dat?" She pointed to the lake. Though it had lightened up, the rain was still drizzling miserably. "And where you going?"

"I . . . I have to go" was Harriet's answer. And then she rose from her seat and entered the house.

"Dis funny kine weather making everybody funny kine, everybody jumpy," Gabriel quipped. He sat pensively, his face as solemn as a doorknob of an old church. Nodding his head, he said, "Dat damn war . . . if it wasn't fo' it, I would be da one making all dis rain instead of suffering from it."

The bit of old-time newspaper that Mary discovered washed upon her shore was the first of many other vintage arrivals. Other newspapers appeared, all soggy and breaking apart, though associative enough to denote the date or style of a time gone by. Even newspapers that were printed in Hawaiian were discovered. The residents of the Hoʻokano house were alarmed at the ominous regularity of the news from the past turning up, which they could not read precisely as the newspapers were in fragments or the ink was bled too weak to be discriminated. And they were also getting more and more isolated from everyone else. The lake was growing like an epidemic and was becoming more or less a lake of dislocation, cutting them off from the rest of Kānewai town.

Come the fifth day and with the rains stopping, the Hoʻokano household began to resist the admonishing touches of despair; they became rejuvenated with the expectation that the lake would recede; and they rose in the morning with the hope that it would take but a short time before life would swing back to normal: driving casually down Kānewai's streets and shopping for specials at Leong's Superette.

But the lake did not recede, and the objects they fished out of the lake were more old newspapers, which were concocting a strange sense of time past and time lost. Their conversations were now tempered with nostalgia. At first they reminisced about happy times but moved invariably towards dark memories that Gabriel, Mary and Harriet had thought were vanquished by over-remembering. They also were running out of food, though the condition did not alarm them since, as they found with the days moving lugubriously on, they were requiring less and less food. (A pot of rice, for example, would last them two to three days.)

But when Kopa began making his first undecipherable sounds, Gabriel was all ears. Like anyone introduced to a strange, new kind of existence, an important part of this incipient experience is to learn the requisite language. In Kopa's case, facility in the moʻo language came quickly since he was a fast learner, though he needed practice to be able to manipulate this new means of communication (he had refused to talk to anyone or any of the other moʻo when he first arrived on the scene). Gabriel and Kopa rekindled a relationship that was marked with the openness and aloha that had distinguished their uncompetitive, unjealous, uncontrived and timeless boyhood years. In the span of one human day, they compressed the love and understanding that should have been theirs during a longer, later period, when both held animosity for one another. (Though Gabriel would deny that he had a feud with his brother, everyone, including Gabriel's inner soul, knew he was a damn liar.)

Gabriel and Kopa at long last were united in blood and soul; their hearts now understood how to weep and rejoice as one. And Gabriel did not stop the relationship from spreading. In fact, he actively shared this new experience with Mary and

Harriet, for he believed—and Kopa did, too—in the importance of sharing the love of loved ones with other loved ones.

Their isolation, then, became a blessing, since they were not distracted by diversions from the community at large. And even the cows were included: They'd eat their fill (the pasture was on higher ground and not affected by encroachment of the lake), then leave through the now unfastened gate and wade through the belly-deep water to the front of the house where they'd spend their time learning, too, this language of isolation.

REBIRTH

They were all hiding their faces from him, these women, sitting on the two long wooden benches in the open-air garage, drawn to old lady Kiyosaki's with the promise that they would be made fertile. Of course, Herman Chung, too, was ashamed, ashamed of being the husband of a woman seeking the old lady's help. He boxed away his embarrassment by bowing his head away from the women, nudging his wife to go ahead of him and take her place at the end of one of the benches. So many things wrong with all these women, he thought. If it's not their headaches, it's the pain in their backs, their periods, their too sensitive—

"Mrs. Oda. Please come in."

A wrinkled-face woman—her thin arms nothing more than leathery skin and blue veins encasing frail bones—called from the back door of the house, then tipped her head to indicate where Mrs. Oda needed to enter.

Mrs. Oda rose quickly, her face pale, and scurried headbent through the doorway, the solid mahogany door closing behind with a brassy snap.

"Ellie, I going," he muttered to his wife, who had taken her place at the end of one bench. The woman next to her had turned away from him. It didn't matter; in fact, he didn't want to look at any of the women straight in the eye, afraid that he'd recognize one of them as perhaps a wife of a friend from work or church.

She turned to him, her face trembling and pallid: Please don't leave me.

"What time I pick you up?"

"I catch the bus," she said, her voice stunted.

"No, I pick you up."

"I catch the bus."

"Ellie—stop it. I pick you up. I come back one hour."

With that, he hurried off.

"What she tol' you?" he asked.

They were heading down Beretania Street, passing the haole church, the Congregational church, with its slate-colored sides and stark white steeple. Two children were playing in a far corner of the church's expansive, well-kept lawn, their parents close by.

"She touched me . . . " She pressed the area of her womb. "She said she feel something good."

"All she like is our money."

"Then why you took me there, then?"

"Never mind."

Ellie turned away and observed the father untangle the line of a colorful samurai kite. The children were watching. The mother was sitting motionless under a shadowless monkey pod. Beyond the steeple, up the valley, dark clouds were suspended, teasing of a hard rain.

"So what she said?"

"What you mean?"

"What she said?" Nervously, he regripped the steering wheel. "Can?"

Ellie held on to the seconds of silence as long as she could. "I tol' you. She said she feel something good."

"But what that mean?"

Ellie glanced out the window. They now were passing the Mormon temple. The statue of Jesus was reaching out a hand. *Give me your blessing, O Lord. Please, O Lord. Jesus' golden face soft and loving.*

"She said can?" Herman repeated.

"Yeah."

Along his side of the road the gray and rosy marble of the Sears and Roebuck building approached. It would be so nice to have a son, he thought. Even a daughter would be okay. Anything. Or both. Can take them bicycle shopping. He took a deep breath and released, as if to assure himself that the ten dollars for the womb massage was worth spending.

"How long she said we gotta wait?"

"She nevah tell me."

"Why you nevah ask?" Fire in his tone. "Chee, why you nevah ask? We pay her dah money, might as well get our money's worth. Why you nevah ask?"

Guiltily, she turned away from him. "I nevah think."

Herman clicked his tongue with disgust. "Ten dollars, and you nevah ask her. No sense you go."

"Eh," she snapped, tossing her guilt for the moment back into his face. "It wasn't my idea." She stabbed him with her eyes. *It's your stinkin' sister*, she thought. *And especially your damn brother-in-law.*

"So what, you blaming my sister?" he said, reading her

mind. "Is not her fault. Is Jin Kuk's fault. He the one. Make my sister that way."

"I nevah say anything." She stared out the windshield. The car came to a stop at a traffic light.

"But das who you blaming. You blaming my sister. Is her husband's fault."

"I not blaming anybody."

"She just speaking her mind. Sometimes she no think before she talk. Stupid, sometimes. But das 'cause Jin Kuk. He dah one."

"But how come you nevah support me when she said that. You my husband. You suppose to back me up. But you nevah say nothing. Nothing. You let her talk what was her mind. So what, she get five kids. So what? What . . . that makes me one failure? You married one failure?"

No sense talking. She get one one-track mind now. One one-track mind.

The light changed to green. He stepped on the gas pedal. They passed the glassed Schumann Carriage showroom where a brand-new Cadillac was rolling out of the company parking lot onto Beretania.

"Sonavabitch haole!" Herman glared at the driver in the Caddy. "Wait til I pass."

The Cadillac stopped. The haole gave Herman a cursing look.

"He think he own the road," Herman spat. "Sonavabitch."

"Watch your temper. He didn't do anything."

"What you mean he nevah do anything?" He looked into the rearview mirror and swore at the driver. "He almost hit us. What you talking about?"

"Nevah mind."

"Whose side you?"

He turned the corner, the air between them thick and ugly. A minute later, they were on their street. Herman drove up the driveway to their cottage converted from a two-car garage. Ellie got out of the car before Herman could apologize for his outburst. He had brought back to her that sorry memory-scar of that evening when Jin Kuk had entered the cottage—as if he owned it—and sat at their small dinner table greedily picking at their food.

Ellie hurries to the kitchen and brings Jin Kuk a plate of rice, leaving the rest in the pot as her portion.

"You have some beer?" Jin Kuk demands in Korean. Herman apologizes that no, he doesn't have any. Jin Kuk grunts in disgust. "You don't even have one bottle of beer to give your oldest brother-in-law?" Glares at Ellie. "What kind of household do you keep here?"

"Where's my sister?" Herman asks in Korean.

"The bitch is in the car. Let her be. She's a pain, always complaining about money. As if I don't make enough!"

"Go get her," Ellie says to Herman in English.

"Leave her alone, that bitch. I should divorce her. All she does is make babies for me, hungry ones that I have to break my damn back every day to feed and clothe."

"Go get her," Ellie insists.

"If you want to see your bitch sister—"

"Don't say that about my sister," Herman says in Korean, his voice wavering.

"Suit yourself."

Herman rises from the table and goes outside. Ellie hears him speaking to Dora in a scolding voice, ordering her to go into the cottage. Dora is refusing him loudly.

"You see what I mean," Jin Kuk tells Ellie, his mouth half-full with food, pointing in the direction with a nod of his head. "What a bitch," he says to himself in English. Then he yells and spits a bit of rice halfway to the doorway. "Get inside here, you bitch! Get inside here right now!"

There is quiet outside, then the sound of the car door opening and slamming shut. Long moments later, Herman enters the cottage, followed by Dora.

He watched Ellie enter the unlocked cottage, her gait strained from the weight of uncertainty and anxiety. He remembered the pain she had in her eyes when Dora had told him that in Korea, if a wife was childless, it was the obligation of the husband to take on a mistress. "She cannot make babee, no good," she had said in English, glancing at Ellie. "In Korea, wife cannot make babee, she no good." Herman had sat there eating his food, looking up only to see Ellie in shock and near tears, then returned to filling his mouth with rice, a sorry excuse for not countering his older sister's thoughtlessly trenchant remark. There were days when he did think about leaving Ellie and finding another woman, a woman with a rich womb, a woman who would give him an heir, a woman with whom he would rejoice at the first buckling steps of a son. Was he to see this, ever?

He got out of the car, reluctant to enter the house that had sentenced him to daily frustration. But perhaps Mrs. Kiyosaki was right. Perhaps they could try again tonight. Perhaps . . .

"Harriet Lindsey called today," Ellie said from inside the screen door of the cottage. Herman was sitting on a chair outside the front door and taking off his work socks.

"Who's that?"

"Harriet. I used to work with her at Fort Ruger."

"The one her husband one cop?"

"Yeah."

She watched him set his work shoes to the side and air his feet, wiggling his toes in the warmth of the late afternoon sun.

"Hard day today?" she asked.

"No. Just tired. Not enough sleep."

He got up and entered the cottage. She followed him to the kitchen sink where he washed his hands, then got a glass of milk from the refrigerator and drank it all in one gulp. There was a lustiness in the way he ate and drank that was attractive to Ellie, something crude but sensual. She waited until he set the empty glass into the sink.

"She told me I should see this Filipino lady," she said, looking out the kitchen window over the small enclosed yard where they sometimes barbecued on the weekends.

"Huh? Whas this for?"

"She said this lady is good. She said right after she saw the Filipino lady, she hāpai. She hāpai five months already."

"One nada soothsayer? How many months already since we wen go the Kiyosaki lady? And what that did? We spend ten dollars for nothing."

"Harriet said this Filipino lady is good. She hāpai. Five months."

"I heard that. So what? You think the Filipino lady, she get magic?"

"I didn't say that. But why not try?"

"You still believe in dis kine magic?"

Herman shook his head. He sat at the kitchen table.

"How much she charge?" he asked.

"Twenty dollars."

"Twenty dollars? How come so pee-sah?"

Ellie rolled her shoulders with uncertainty.

"Twenty dollars," Herman mused. "Dis is one racket, these old ladies. Trying make one buck off people who need something."

He studied Ellie, who had sat down in the chair across from him, her head bent and her chest sunken. She's beautiful, he thought, but why she gotta have something wrong with her? He thought of his former girlfriend whom he was supposed to marry ten years back, who was now married to his best friend. They just had their third child, a daughter.

"Okay," he mumbled. "Le's go. You know how contact her?"

Ellie looked up, her eyes with a touch of hope, albeit a desperate one. "Yeah. Harriet gave me her phone number." She handed him the folded scrap of paper that was on the table.

He read the five-digit number. "Where this stay?"

"She said she live Damon Tract."

Herman nodded his head. "Well, if you think going help. Call her up today. Right now."

"I did. She wants us come Saturday, day time."

He nodded his head, then slid back his chair and went to the bathroom to shower off his filth.

A heavy rain had come down over Puʻuloa but had ceased suddenly when they came to Nimitz Highway and its row of used and new car dealers. Herman drove down Lagoon Drive, that two-lane road that led to the territorial airport, and took a right turn onto a dirt road. There was a sudden dip in the road, which forced Herman to brake almost to a stop, fearing that they might plunge over a cliff. At the top of the dip, the road leveled off and meandered through an area of stark kiawe trees and dried buffalo grass. The road wound its way for a hundred yards or so to the soothsayer's house, an old small house built in plantation workers' style with a flat, corrugated-iron roof painted a marbleized avocado green. The walls of the house were vermillion in color, the trim navy blue, and the surrounding picket fence a Kaiser pink. Herman noticed the meticulous upkeep of the house, in sharp contrast to the run-down state of the other sparsely scattered cottages they had passed, and the small yard was neatly trimmed and without a stray leaf on the ground.

Ellie pointed to a dry spot next to the fence, and Herman pulled over to it. He cut the engine, took out the key, then rein-serted it in the ignition. Finally, he looked at a nervous Ellie and said, "Le's go."

They pushed open the gate, and an old poi bitch arose from the shadows underneath the house and greeted them with squinting eyes and a wagging tail. She came up to Herman and offered him her head, but Herman shooed her away. "Get away dog! Pilau, you!"

"She clean," a tired voice from the porch balcony pro-claimed. An elderly Filipino woman sat in a rocking chair smoking a pipe. Herman could smell the harsh odor of tobacco. She took a couple of puffs, then leaned forward. "What you here fo'?"

"We looking fo' Mrs. Ginaca," Ellie said.

"Das me. Whachu like?"

"I call you yesterday and you tol' me fo' come over. About . . . my condition." Ellie rubbed her stomach nervously.

The old woman nodded her head. "Yas, I remembah. You said you like me help you make keiki." She gave Ellie a look over. "You look healthy. What you, Japanee?"

"Korean."

"Koh-rean," the old woman said with a kind of finality, as if she had made a decision. She looked at Herman, her eyes enlarging and bloodshot and glazed. "You pay me first. Twenty-five dollars."

Herman's jaw dropped. "But you tol' my wife twenty dollars."

The old woman puffed on her pipe and raised a hand, palm upward, as if to say, "Take it or leave it."

"Plus, five dollars for weekend fee," she added. "Thirty dollahs altogethah."

"Thirty dollars. Eh, dis is highway—" He cut short his comment. Ellie was melting between them, partly from embarrassment, partly from helplessness. Herman looked to the ground, then reached into his back pocket and pulled out his worn brown wallet. He opened it and counted thirty-one dollars. He carefully lifted thirty dollars and left the one dollar, a silver certificate that he had been holding on to for several years, hoping that the old woman had not seen it. He returned the wallet to his back pocket, stepped up to the porch, and spread out the money, fanlike, and gave it to the old woman.

The old woman counted the money, then rolled it up and stuffed it in a leather pouch that was attached to her side by a cord around her waist. She nodded her head at Ellie and stood up.

"Come," she said, and opened the screen door, signaling Ellie to enter. Ellie and Herman followed the old woman, but the old woman stopped Herman. "You . . . you wait us'side," she said, pointing to the rocking chair. She summoned Ellie into the house again.

Herman sat on the chair, which reeked of tobacco, his mind swirling with anger, his hands twitching and cold from frustration. It didn't feel good, this encounter with the Filipino lady. It didn't feel good at all. He and Ellie were getting robbed again. Thirty bucks. Almost an entire week's pay.

The dog crept shyly up to Herman, begging for some affection. But Herman sent her scampering off. "Get lost, you bitch! Beat it!"

He looked out at the landscape. The old lady kept a lot of green plants and flowers and several huge kalamungai trees. Just beyond the fence, the landscape was barren except for the kiawe trees thirsting for moisture. Even with the hard rain that had come down, the ground and trees had sucked up every drop of water and still it looked as if it hadn't rained at all. But that was funny: Herman noticed that the wide green leaves of the ti plants, which surrounded the house, were splattered with rain.

He waited and waited. He heard noises inside the house that sounded like furniture being dragged about. Outside, the only sounds were the muffled dark buzzings of airplanes landing and lifting off at the airport, and the occasional distant horns of the cargo ships in the channel. He then realized that he had not heard a dog bark or the chirping of a bird at all. Nothing. It was as if by Ellie entering the house, the soothsayer had ordered all animal life to cease to exist. Even the old dog had vanished.

Herman looked at his watch. A half an hour had passed in silence since he heard those dragging sounds. He needed to urinate. He peered through the screen door. The interior was dark, and the living room was spartan: he could see only a worn stuffed chair and a small kitchen table with three wooden chairs. The scent of bagoong wafted to him, lifting his nostrils and eyebrows. He called out, but his hellos seemed to be muted by the thickness of the air. He couldn't wait. He had to urinate. He went to the side of the house and started to relieve himself in a wet thicket of ti.

A soft chanting, in a language he could not understand, came from behind the bush. Must be Filipino, he said to himself. He finished and zipped himself, but instead of returning to the front, he stood still and listened to the droning rhythm of the chant. Stepping to the side of his puddle, he slipped into the bush, careful not to make a disturbance. The chanting rose in pitch, then subsided, then rose again and lowered to a rumbling, prickling his skin. Through a few leaves he saw the flickering of candles. He cleared away the leaves, which gave him a clear view inside a bedroom window. His eyes widened in horror. Choking on his saliva, he fought back the urge to cough.

Ellie was floating a foot above a bed with several burning candles balanced on her bared midriff. Her eyes were closed as if in a deep sleep, and her arms, hanging limply, were twitching. With her eyes also closed and eyelids fluttering, the old woman continued to chant while rubbing a string of black beads. And when her eyes suddenly opened to his, he felt something enter his body and wrestle with his blood. He tumbled backwards, his arms flailing against the stiffening and flagellating leaves, desperately trying to grab onto anything to prevent his fall into a roaring vortex.

"Herman . . . Herman . . . wake up."

His eyes opened to Ellie's apologetic face.

"Sorry it took so long. C'mon. Le's go home."

He bolted up from the rocking chair, blood rushing from his head. Dizzily, he collapsed back into the chair. After a minute, with the pounding in his head clearing somewhat, he realized where he was. His clothes were damp. This time he stood up slowly. The old woman was leaning against the doorjamb, holding open the screen door. She was smiling and puffing on her pipe. The odor of the tobacco was nauseating.

"Herman, you must've wen fall asleep," Ellie said. "Sorry it took so long."

"Das okay," he said. He glanced at the woman, but withdrew his eyes quickly, grabbed Ellie's hand and led her down the steps.

"Wait, Herman." Ellie pulled her hand out of his grip and turned, thanking the old woman. He turned from the house, his head bent.

The old woman nodded her head with a smile and through pursed lips said, "Remembah what I say."

Ellie acknowledged her with a weak smile and thanked her again.

Herman's heart was trying to punch itself out of his body as he backed out the car and straightened it down the dirt driveway. He glanced back at the house through the rearview mirror, but the old woman had already gone in. The dog was sitting at the gate, its tail resting motionless on the ground, its eyes alertly watching them leave.

"Whas the matter, Herman?"

"Nothing."

"You sure you okay?"

"Yeah . . . yeah . . . I okay. Le's go home."

After the first turn in the road, his heart began to settle down.

"Can we get something to eat? I paeg-go-pah."

"Yeah—yeah."

"Herman, you okay?"

"Yeah . . . yeah. What you like eat?"

"You get money?"

"Yeah . . . I get. I get my silver certificate."

"But I thought you like save that?"

"Nevah mind. What you like eat?"

"Anything."

They rode in silence. Herman drove the car up the steep incline to Lagoon Drive, headed towards Nimitz, then crossed the highway to Puʻuloa.

"Where you going, Herman?" Ellie asked, looking back.

"Huh?"

"You just pass one market."

"Oh."

"Herman, you okay?"

"Yeah."

"You want to know what she told me?"

Herman took a deep breath. "Yeah."

Ellie pressed her stomach. "She said . . . she said my womb is cold. She touch my stomach. She lomi-lomi some oil on top. She said my womb is cold. But she said going be all right."

"Going be . . . all right?"

"Das what she said."

"Going be all right," he whispered, looking out his window for a moment. He released a heavy sigh.

A sudden rain came down. A cold damp air rushed into the car.

"Yeah, das what she said," Ellie said, rolling up her window. "She said going be all right."

HAE SOON'S SONG

"What you have to do," Suzy said matter-of-factly in Korean, "is let them feel your breasts." She sipped her soft drink through a thin plastic straw, then gazed across the empty dance floor, humming a few bars of Bruce Springsteen's "Dancing in the Dark." "But what they really like is when you fondle them."

Hae Soon, sitting across the table from Suzy, bowed her head in embarrassment.

"Let them touch you a little, just enough," Suzy continued, like a well-meaning older sister. "Otherwise, they'll order one drink and leave for another place. Or worst yet, they'll give their business to one of the *other* girls." She glared at the bar where the other hostesses were gathered.

With a tilt of her head, Suzy tossed ringlets of her lightened hair from one side of her face to the other. "And why don't you go to a hairdresser and have something done to your hair? You look like a little school girl." She waited for an answer. There was none. She shook her head. "I don't get it. I don't know why you want to work here. You've worked here for a week and all you're doing is wasting your time, your money. You haven't made enough even to tip the bar and housemother or to pay the taxi fare home."

"I'm managing," Hae Soon answered quickly, also in Korean. "And I don't have to—"

"And who are you calling cheap? Not me, I hope."

"I didn't say that."

"But that's what you were going to say. Just remember that I'm showing you all this because our families come from the same province. I don't have to do this, you know."

Hae Soon lowered her eyes. "No, I didn't mean it that way," she said.

Hanging from the ceiling, a rotating disco ball was showering the dance floor with spots of bright light.

Hae Soon turned towards the bar and regarded Jimmy Choi, the tired-eyed bartender, who was leaning against the cash register and watching the television set mounted from the ceiling. His baggy eyes, his sagging cheeks—*he looks like one of those fat-faced house dogs—what did they call them?—beagles?—the kind of dog that the American colonel's wife always brought into father's shop?* She read the time on the clock, then returned to Suzy, but only for a moment, afraid that Suzy might unleash her terrible temper again. Yes, she should be fortunate that Suzy had gotten her the job. Jobs were hard to find in Hawai'i, especially if one is an immigrant with very limited English.

But she never imagined that she would be a bargirl.

They were outcasts, treated like dirt, those women in the doorways.

On the way home from school to her father's modest tailor shop that was tucked in a narrow alley in downtown Seoul, she would pass the clubs with brassy music pouring out of the door-

ways. Those doorways that smelled of rice wine and perfume.
On slow days, the girls would gather out front, their glossy tight
skirts with slits on the sides showing their sleek white thighs,
their cheeks powdered and lips painted red. And when they
saw Hae Soon or any of her school girlfriends, they'd call out,
"Pretty little girl! Ah! Pretty little girl!" Then, one day, one of
the bargirls befriended Hae Soon—her name was Min Ja—and
Min Ja gave Hae Soon a piece of wheat candy. The next day
Min Ja called Hae Soon to an empty stool next to the doorway. Hae Soon sat, and they talked about Hae Soon's school,
about Min Ja's home in Kwangju—they talked about Min Ja's
picking of ripened persimmons and her grandmother making
honeyed rice cakes—and they talked until the long shadows
of passersby suggested the coming of darkness. And when Hae
Soon arrived at her father's shop, she received a terrible scolding. But Hae Soon returned to that doorway and Min Ja, who
always had a stool and a candied treat for her. And then one
time Min Ja quietly began braiding Hae Soon's hair, and after
a while Hae Soon glanced back and saw that tears were in Min
Ja's eyes, her eyes were blackening, dark streams of tears were
dripping down her cheeks. *Why are Min Ja's tears black?*

*They're bad women, her mother told her, don't even think of
looking in there. And never walk past there again. Do you know
what people will say if they see you there? Do you? Do you?! If
you go past there again, I will tell your father.*

So she stopped walking that route from school, for a long
while. But one day she passed that doorway again. Every day
she had thought about her friend Min Ja, and she missed her
friend: the way Min Ja combed and braided her hair, her stories of her childhood, her soft pleasant voice. Hae Soon heard
American rock 'n roll music blaring out of the dark doorway.
She slowed her walk to a stop and stared into the establish-

ment, which she had never entered, squinting her eyes at the loud and abusive music that made her ears ring. Before she could call for Min Ja, one of the other girls came out and greeted Hae Soon. *Are you looking for Min Ja? Lucky girl! She's gone off and gotten married to a rich man.*

Hae Soon ran from there, as fast as the flight of a newspaper down a gusty downtown street, *as fast as the frolicking run of a mountain stream, running over slippery rocks,* past crocks and carts of food, past the vendor tables of bright goods, *past the darting fish,* past the scattering cats of smelly trash heaps. She didn't know why she was running. Was it because she was afraid to be caught dead in front of that house of the dark doorway? Was it because Min Ja had left without telling her? And when she was a good distance away, a block from her father's shop, she ran into a dirty, urine-smelling alley, leaned her head against the brick wall and cried.

"Look at her! Look at her, Hae Soon! Hae Soon? Hae Soon?! Look at her . . . there, at the bar. Last month she wasn't that big. Oh, my! No wonder I haven't seen her all this time. Where did she get the money to get those breasts? Her boyfriend, probably. She did it for him. Yes. He's an attorney. Hmph! So who cares?!"

Hae Soon surveyed the girl in the low-cut red evening dress. She sipped her Coke and brought her hands together on her lap, forming a folded fan.

"You know," Suzy said, narrowing her eyes, "I introduced her to him. And she took him away from me. He was *my* boyfriend."

He was a poet. His name was Yong Gil. She met him at the university where he was student of literature and modern poetics. He was young and brilliant, handsome and brave. He wrote poetry that was powerful and beautiful, each word full with lifemeaning. One day, a month after they had been going together, he presented her with a book of poems, each poem a love ode to her. He explained to her that the book was two years in the making, the time he had endured a distant, feverish love for her.

And he wrote other poems, of course, mainly poems of his great love for legendary Kumgangsan—the Diamond Mountains—though he had never seen them, since the mountains were part of the prohibited North. *The mountains are brave mountains,* Yong Gil told her. *Kumgangsan is like the Korean people, standing strong and battling invaders and destroyers of everything Korean.*

It was romantic, being with Yong Gil. Romantic.

Her father did not like him. Yong Gil was too outspoken: he openly criticized the Chun Do Hwan government as being a fascist dictatorship and a puppet of American imperialism. He was a known subversive. He had been arrested one, maybe two or three times. But Hae Soon could not listen to her father: she was in love with Yong Gil and his vision of Kumgangsan. At those secret student meetings, she watched Yong Gil speak, her eyes fixed on him, her face like a flower opening to a morning sun. And in the bitter, long winter nights, their bodies as one melted the ice of the air.

"Let's go dancing tonight," Suzy said, her voice flat. She began humming the popular Korean song that was now playing on the jukebox, the song about the Man with the Yellow Shirt:

I don't know why, but I like him,
That Man with the Yellow Shirt.

I don't know why, but I like him,
That Man with the Yellow Shirt.

Hae Soon stared at Suzy, her thoughts of Yong Gil vanishing into the dark, empty atmosphere. "Yes? What is it?"

"There you go again," Suzy grumbled. "Always in your dream cloud. That's why the other girls out-hustle you all the time. That, plus you don't put out. Do you really want to work here?"

Hae Soon straightened up. "Have some customers come in?"

"No—no—silly! How are we going to have customers on a dead night like tonight?" She looked away, shaking her head. "Look. Let's go dancing tonight. We could go down to Seoul Palace. I know the bartender there. He and I used to work at the Bluebird Lounge on Keʻeaumoku. He's really nice. And he has a cute brother working with him. Maybe I could introduce you . . . "

Hae Soon shook her head.

"Oh! You're no fun!" Suzy folded her arms over her chest and sank as low as she could in her seat. "I don't know why you work here. All you do is sit around and sip your Coke. And dream. How do you expect to make a living in Hawaiʻi? And you with a child to support. You have to hustle. Work hard. Oh . . . I don't know why I talk to you."

Hae Soon's eyes moistened. Gently she dabbed her eyes with a paper napkin so as not to smear the mascara.

"Oh, I'm sorry," Suzy offered. "You know me. When it gets slow like tonight, I get this way. You're my friend. Our families come from the same province. It's like we know each other for a long time. Right?" She paused to check on an entering customer. Without looking around, the older local Asian man sat at the bar. "Look. I'm sorry I told you these things. All right? You forgive me?"

Hae Soon forced a smile and nodded her head. "It's all right. I know . . . I've . . . I've been stubborn."

"We're all like that. And we're all in this same disgusting boat. *Aiigoo!*"

"Maybe we can go dancing tonight?"

Suzy's eyes lit up. "All right . . . if you want to. And I'll introduce you to Tong Sul's cute brother."

Hae Soon waved off the matchmaking suggestion, shaking her head. "No—no arrangement. All right? Please?"

"You're still in love with him, aren't you?"

Hae Soon nodded, a shy smile rising to her face.

"Oh . . . come on," Suzy said, taking Hae Soon's hand. "You can be honest with me. I can understand. I was in love once, too." Suzy's eyes became distant. She let Hae Soon's hand go. "Sometimes . . . I wonder what is it like to be in love again. It's been such a long time." Suzy's eyes reached across the dance floor for the country love song playing on the jukebox. "What is his name again?"

"Yong Gil."

It was spring, and they had eloped. It was a beautiful time of the year. The air was warm and the earth fecund, and the blossoms on the apple and persimmon trees threw their ripe redolence into the air. And those wonderfully romantic and hectic days of love and lust and demonstrations against the ruling order lasted for all that spring and into an eruptive summer.

They had fallen asleep after a night of lovemaking when the police broke down their door. They beat a bewildered, naked and struggling Yong Gil, then handcuffed him. They grabbed her womanparts and came near raping her with their batons in front of Yong Gil with his mouth of broken teeth when their professor friend, from whom they rented the small cottage, came storming out of the main house and demanded that the police leave immediately. They threw Hae Soon down on the floor, even with her showing five months, and started on the professor, slashing a baton across his face, then smashing his face into a whimpering mess. But they left without further touching her: maybe they were overdue at the station, perhaps they had to hustle up more radicals for their nightly quota. *Those dogs! They dragged Yong Gil clutching only a blanket for cover.*

"Yong Gil," Suzy mused. "That's a nice name. Of course, he must be very handsome. You say he is very smart, too?"

Yong Gil. I will love no one else but you. Forever.

Willow weeps like a thousand cranes
With heads bowed
And legs crossed:
A hunger for fish they feel.
We hide under its branches,
Hear its weeping
And feel our hunger
Cursed from birth.

But far away loom majestic mountains
Of diamond spires and sides of jade
And topped with emeralds.
We may be careless,
Wounded birds of love,
Pushed to and fro by cold harsh winds,
But when we reach the jeweled mountains,
The ugly scars from hate
Will disappear.

We'll love again:
Love seeds new love.

"What did you say?" Suzy asked, her eyes wide with curiosity.

"Huh? Oh . . . Yong Gil. His name is Yong Gil."

"Yes, you told me that. But what was it you were saying after that?"

"Oh, I don't know." Hae Soon shook her head with embarrassment. "I don't remember."

Suzy frowned. "All right, you don't have to tell me. But tell me this. Why did you come to Hawai'i where there are no good jobs? The only thing a woman can do here is to work in a bar."

"I told you before."

"But I want to hear it again. Besides, what else is there to talk about? Is there any excitement in our lives?" Suzy spun a hard look over the crowdless room.

"I had to leave," Hae Soon said, biting her words.

"But you said you were a high school teacher. You had a good job in Seoul. You leave a good job to come here to make money hustling in a bar? You had a future in Korea. And anyway, what good is a teacher in America who can't speak English?"

"Let's go dancing tonight!"

Suzy threw her hands in the air. "All right. If you don't want to talk about it. You just get me all upset. You don't even confide in me. After all, I'm your only friend in Hawai'i."

Yes, a good friend in Hawai'i. But you wouldn't understand.
You can't understand.

A customer staggered into the lounge, an old gray man, local Oriental. Immediately Suzy jumped up to greet him before the other girls could slide off their stools. Holding the old man's hand, she led him to a dim corner of the lounge and sat him down. Shortly after, she ordered at the bar, plunked a few quarters into the jukebox and made her selection of popular Japanese songs. Then she glided over to Hae Soon.

"The old man says that his friends are going to join him in a little while. When they come, join us. I've been with them before. They like to touch a lot, but they're big spenders."

Hae Soon watched Suzy's lean swaying hips as she sashayed to the bar to pick up the order.

Maybe I should walk like her. No. What am I saying?

She regarded the large digital clock behind the bar. Time was hardly passing tonight. And how long ago was it when she left Korea and Yong Gil? Seven months ago? A year? Ten years?

Why did she leave?

That ancient bronze bell used to resound over the university campus, signaling the end of the class period. She would wait for him down by the ancient royal fishponds, and there they'd walk hand in hand, something they couldn't do in public. And the nights they'd spend locked up in one of the stuffy study rooms in the library: alone, trusting, warm skin on warm skin.

Oh, Yong Gil! Why did they take you away? Do you think about our son? How we live our lives so—

"Hae Soon! Hae Soon!" Suzy shook Hae Soon on the shoulder. "What's the matter with you?"

Hae Soon straightened up and blinked, startled by Suzy's round, piercing eyes.

"Come on, Hae Soon. His friends are here. Quickly—before the others beat you to them!"

Hae Soon fumbled for her handbag—*oh, it's behind the bar, I forgot*—then sidled out of the booth. Straightening her dress borrowed from Suzy's copious and silky wardrobe, she followed her friend obediently, past empty booths to the carousing men. Suzy glanced over her shoulders, gave Hae Soon a look of warning, then wiggled and smiled and laughed as she joined the men, settling herself between two of them.

Hae Soon found herself smiling. And, mildly surprised that the effort was easier than she thought, she was copying Suzy's waltzing steps. The noticing men rejoiced with her arrival. One of them flashed his gold teeth, which shone dull and warm in the semi-darkness. Hae Soon sat down in the booth across from Suzy. The table was covered with bottles of beer and platters of food. She poured beer into the glass of the strongly cologne-scented man sitting next to her.

"What's your name?" the man asked.

"My nam-ah? Oh—Hae Soon."

"No!" interrupted Suzy, emphatically shaking her head, then smiling. "Her name ez—her name ez—eh—Eva."

"How are you, Eva?" the man said with a smile. "How come you dunno yo' name?" The men laughed. "Eva, how 'bout you bring me and my friends one 'nother round?"

"Go to Jimmy and order three Budweisers," Suzy interpreted in Korean.

Hae Soon nodded her head and went to the bar. She gave the order to Jimmy Choi, then turned to the other hostesses and smiled. They were whispering among themselves, avoiding eye contact with her. Hae Soon paid Jimmy, then returned to the table with the order.

Suzy was in the arms of the grayish man, playfully diverting his hands from entering the openings of her dress.

Hae Soon looked away and served the beer. The strongly scented man patted the empty seat next to him. Reluctantly, she sat down, folding her arms across her chest.

"You pretty," the man said. "How long you stay here in Hawai'i?"

She shrugged her shoulders. Suzy tapped Hae Soon in the shin with the toe of her shoe, then translated the question into Korean.

"Oh—I t'ink so—fo' month—soo—already."

"You speak good English. My friends and me, all the time we come dis bar, but first time we see you. How long you been working here?"

She nodded, not understanding what he had said.

He put his arm around her shoulders. Hae Soon shivered. "You have beautiful skin." He ran his hand up and down her arm.

Hae Soon looked at Suzy for help, but the grayish man's hand was all over Suzy's chest now, and Suzy's hand was lowered somewhere in his groin, out of Hae Soon's view. She closed her eyes, wishing she was imagining what she was seeing. Then the man next to her slipped his hand under her arms. She resisted, shaking off the advance. He grinned, snickered, and pursued more, his other hand gripping her outside shoulder, bringing her tighter into his snare. She refused him, but finally, finally, she let him in, loosening the lock of her arms though not dropping them. The man found a breast and squeezed it. It hurt her. He kissed her on the cheek, his alcoholic breath burning her skin, that thick cologne smell rubbing off on her face. She trembled. She fought back a cry.

"You're very pretty."

"I— come back—hokay?"

"No," the man said, holding her down. "I like you here. You stay here and take care of me, and I take care of you." He pointed with his eyes to a small pile of money at the edge of the table.

Suzy was laughing. "Isn't this fun?" she said in Korean. "This old man is so small, but he's so funny."

The men finished their beers and asked for another round. Hae Soon leaped out of the booth, straightening her bra, and went to the bar before Suzy could unstrap the gray man's arms. She put in the order. The girls on the stools were giggling at her. Embarrassed, Hae Soon looked the other way, towards the open front door. It was raining outside. She thought of walking out.

They were walking in the rain the day she told him she was pregnant. He was silent for a long while, his face furrowed with anxiety. Then, suddenly, he leaped ahead of her, jumping up and down while clapping his hands and shouting to the world, "I'm going to be a father! I'm going to be a father!" He dropped to his knees and begged her to marry him.

She could not answer. She was crying. She had never seen Yong Gil so deliriously happy. It shook her. But she took his wet head and pressed it against her womb.

Can you feel our baby breathe, my love?
Can you feel our baby move?
Can you hear the beating heart
Like wings fluttering,
A thousand doves
Descending from the Heavens?

Hae Soon glanced back at the booth. Suzy was laughing with the men. Hae Soon didn't want to return. But the money. The money.

His face was battered, though his eyes were alert and filled with anger.

"Yong Gil!!"

"Shut up, whore! Hurry up! Get him out of here."

"And the other?" Pointing to the professor unconscious on the ground.

"Leave him. Hurry up! Let's go!"

His mouth opened, but his words were broken, unspeakable. He spat out a bloody tooth, then another. Coughed. In desperation he made weak gestures—his hands, arms, head—trying to convey the message to her: *Stomach?—Baby?—Are you all right?*

They handcuffed him and dragged him out the door on his bare ass.

Yong Gil, please understand. It's all for little Yong Gil, little one. So he can grow up big and strong, return home to find his father. And he'll get back at them, those bastards, sons of bastard pigs, for humiliating his father—

"Hae Soon?! What are you doing?" Suzy. "They're waiting and waiting for their drinks. Are you dreaming again?"

"I—I'm coming."

"And call yourself *Eva*. Don't you like that name?"

Jimmy Choi stared at her, then grinned at the other girls: What's wrong with this bitch?

"Oh—yes—"

"Come on. They're waiting." Suzy scurried back to the table.

Hae Soon paid the bartender, then hurried back to the booth.

"How come took you so long?" the cologne man asked. Hae Soon forced a smile.

The man said something to his friend. They looked at her and grinned.

"Charlie says he like to date you," the man said. "But I tol' him fo' get lost. You mine tonight, eh, sweetheart?"

The man smiled broadly, showing his gold teeth. He corralled her with a large arm and kissed her on the cheek. He tried to touch her breast again, but Hae Soon pushed his thick calloused hands away. He forced his hand up her dress and grabbed her crotch. She shrieked, squirmed out of his grasp and jumped out of the booth, then grabbed an empty bottle from the table and broke it on his face.

"Hae Soon!!"

· She grabbed the money and threw it at the men.

Suzy leaped out of her seat and tangled her arms with Hae Soon's. "Stop it!! Hae Soon!!"

The bottle had cut the man's cheek. Blood was streaming out of the wound. With anger and disbelief, the man stared at the blood dripping on his hand, then cautiously touched his face. He lunged out of the booth.

"You cunt!"

He grabbed Suzy, who was in the way, by the hair and tossed her to the side, where she fell like a crumpled puppet.

"You cunt!"

A blow sent Hae Soon flying into another table. The man lifted her and beat her with an open hand until Jimmy Choi and the man's drinking partners could restrain him.

"You cunt!"

From the floor, numb with pain, she watched the struggle, the commotion, the madness, as if she were an outsider looking in. Two girls from the bar began mothering her, trying to help her up. She pushed them away, then shakily pulled herself up. She grabbed her handbag from the back of the bar and started towards the door. But she stopped halfway across the dance floor. With the swirling spots of light covering her, she glared at the dogs, spat at them, then marched out of the lounge.

The rain had stopped. The air was cool. The boulevard was empty of cars. She gazed at the dark sky and took a deep breath before taking off her shoes and nylons. A block from the lounge a taxi slowed down beside her. She waved it away. She had no money for a cab, nothing for food and rent that was due in another week. How could she and little Yong Gil survive? On Yong Gil's thin volume of poetry? On sympathy from the dogs?

I don't know why but I like him,
That Man with the Yellow Shirt.
I don't know why but I like him,
That Man with the Yellow Shirt.

AN ANGEL FOR GUY MATSUZAKI

"How long mo' you get befo' you pau wit' da schoolteachah's car?"

Guy Matsuzaki carefully pushed himself out from under the hood of the car he was working on, holding a greasy socket wrench in his right hand. "I dunno, Naka," he answered. "Maybe half hour. Maybe one hour."

"Finish up da job befo' you go home. Da schoolteachah going come in early Monday morning pick up da car." Naka was cleaning his hands with a couple of paper towels.

"Yeah. Okay, Naka."

Guy remembered the schoolteacher. Japanese. Perhaps a few years younger than him. Pretty. She looked him straight in the eye and described in perfect English the problem she had experienced with her car. He could not meet her eyes when he was explaining what he thought was wrong. Later her boyfriend picked her up in his shiny red sports car.

"I going home already. When you pau wit' da job, clean up and close up da shop, eh?"

"Okay, Naka."

"And no forget close da light in da bathroom. Dis morning I found da light on. My electricity bill going up and up every month."

"Okay, Naka."

"I see you Monday."

"Yeah. Good night."

The owner of the garage tossed the balled paper towels into an old oil barrel that served as a rubbish receptacle. "Good night," he said, the tone of his voice dropping. He wiggled his thick body through the narrow opening of the accordion-like garage door. He poked his head back in. "Eh, remember close up da shop good. I no like nobody running off wit' my tools."

"Yeah, Naka."

"And da lights," Naka reminded, finally leaving the shop.

Guy didn't answer. He gazed at the clock on the wall, its face filmed with years of greasy dust. Seven-seventeen P.M. The job—the replacement of a fuel pump—would take him another twenty, no more than twenty-five minutes. He'd have to clean up the area and that would take about twenty minutes, but if he pushed himself, maybe fifteen. He was anxious to get out. Naka had paid him today, and it being a Friday, he was in a rush to get to the Paradise Lounge. He had read in Tuesday evening's sports section that three new girls were dancing there, and that news gave him something to look forward to for the rest of the week. He had sweated it out all day today, relieved that Naka didn't ask him—order him—to come in on Saturday. Besides, business had been dropping for the past couple of months, which was the probable reason why Naka had been so grouchy for the past week or so.

Guy adjusted the work light, then went back to the stubborn nut. The way they designed engines nowadays was ass-backwards. In order to get into a position to remove and replace this particular nut, he had to place his socket wrench beneath the pump at an awkward angle. But finally the nut was tightened. He relinked the hoses and wires, reconnected the negative cable to the battery, and turned the key in the ignition a notch to get the pump going. Then he started the engine. It kicked up fine. While the car idled for a few minutes, he cleared away the tools and wiped the fender clean, then checked for leaks. Satisfied, he got into the car and parked it further into the garage, killing the engine and leaving the key in the ignition. He wrote up the work order and left it in the tray on Naka's messy desk. Then he cleaned up the rest of the garage.

By 7:55 P.M. he was out, closing the garage door. But just as he was about to lock it, he flashed on Naka's nagging complaint concerning the bathroom light. He thought he had switched if off but wasn't completely sure. Swearing, he pushed through the narrow opening of the folding door, checked on the bathroom and found the light off, then returned to closing up the garage.

It felt good to close the shop without the boss around and finally enter the comfort zone of his car. The '55 Chevy started with hardly an effort, the engine whining like a steady breeze through tall grass. He tapped the accelerator pedal once, two times, and waited until the warming engine lost that hint of hesitation. Then he backed out of his stall and drove home.

His mother was watching television when he entered the house. "Yo' dinner getting cold," she said, her eyes not leaving the set.

"Going eat out tonight."

"Why you nevah call me up earlier and let me know?"

He mumbled something about how she should know by

now that every Friday he went out on the town. He crossed the living room without looking at her and entered his bedroom, got a change of underwear, and went to take a shower. Fifteen minutes later he emerged from a steamy bathroom smelling of soap and aftershave. Closing his door, he finished dressing, choosing a pair of black slacks and a long-sleeved knit shirt. Using the mirror mounted on the back of the door, he combed his hair and checked to see if his moustache was neatly trimmed, then opened his wallet to count his pay. Two hundred twenty-three dollars. Twenty-three dollars he tucked with the few other dollars he had under a pile of worn car and girlie magazines next to his bed. His gas and lunch money for the following week. Then he stole past his mother to the kitchen.

"What time you coming home?" his mother asked.

He didn't answer. He counted seventy-five dollars and left it on the kitchen table. No need to tell her that the money was hers. In the morning it would be gone. He started out the front door.

"What time you coming home? Late?"

This time he answered. "Late."

"Come home early. Get too many accidents nowadays. Too many drunk drivers. I heard on the radio dis morning, had one terrible accident by the . . . "

He left the house and her talking. It was the same thing repeated every time he went out. He was thirty-five-years old, thirty-six in three months, and still she treated him like a child. He wanted to move out, to be on his own, but he knew he would never do it. For now, he'd just ignore her talk, give her money, and continue with his routine. He knew that she'd probably stay up for him till midnight, when he'd still be barhopping. And when he came home in the early morning hours, that dismal yellow lamp in the corner of the living room would be on. He'd creep into his bedroom and his mother would call out in a clear but tentative voice, "Dat you, Guy?" He'd pause, then as was expected, give a drunken grunt, his way of answering that yes, he was home. And that would be that. He'd plop in bed and sleep a dreamless sleep.

The parking lot of the lounge was full. He had to park down the street, but that was okay since later he'd wander off to another of the dozen bars in the area. Or maybe he'd meet a girl tonight and go out for a fun time. Or, if he met an old friend, he'd go driving off to another concentration of bars in some other part of town. But that was getting rarer, since most of his old classmates were married and raising kids or expecting them, and their wives kept them home. Those were good lives they had, and he envied them. After graduation, with the help of his mother's friend, he had gotten a job at Naka's Garage, thinking that he was doing the right thing. The rest of his friends had gone to trade school or entered the service. A couple of them went to the state university. Those were the days when he always seemed to have more money than his friends, and often he was the one treating when they drank at bars. But now, with most of them holding good jobs, the reciprocal treatment was not in effect. Except that one time he met Henry Matsumoto, who had had a fight with his wife and had taken off to the hostess bars to cool off. He saw Henry at the Red Rose Lounge, and they began buying each other beers while trading stories from the old days. From there they barhopped until about three in the morning. After breakfast at a drive-in, they exchanged phone numbers, promising to call each other for another night out on the town. Henry never called, so Guy called two weeks later, but the number Henry gave was disconnected.

Tonight, more likely, he'd wander to two or three bars by himself, then call it a night with the last call.

Guy entered the noisy Paradise Lounge. On a square stage a tall slender blonde was go-go dancing to a Donna Summer tune, her small pointed breasts bouncing to the beat. Seated around the stage were men, mostly local, their eyes affixed on the dancer's pale flesh, a couple of them persuading her to take off more. She seemed pleased at the attention of a handful of admirers who were slipping one-dollar bills under her G-string. She must be one of the new girls they advertised about, Guy thought.

A Korean hostess whom he had also never seen before approached him and asked if he wanted to be seated. She was pretty, dressed in a tight black dress that exposed the tops of her breasts. Her eyes met his. For a moment, induced by the dim lights, Guy thought he saw a quiet yearning in her eyes. But he looked away, nodding his head, yes, he wanted to be seated. He was never able to look into a woman's eyes for more than a moment.

The hostess led him to a seat on the side of the stage, next to two men who were dressed like himself. He ordered a beer and turned his attention to the performance. The dancer turned up her act, slipping down her G-string just enough to show a bit of pubic hair, then raising it back up.

The Korean hostess returned with his order and a small bowl of salted peanuts. She poured the beer into a small tumbler. Again Guy would not look into her face, but he watched her slender hands do their job. On one finger, the gemstone of a ring shone brilliantly in sparkles of red, blue and yellow. He paid her, thanked her and gave her a small tip, then sipped the beer.

The men next to Guy began hooting and shouting as the

entire lounge caught on fire with the dancer's performance. Her G-string was down to her ankles now, and she continued on with her routine that gave the men teasing glimpses of her crotch. And then she was finished, smiling as she picked up the money showered on the stage. The two men next to Guy made airplanes out of dollar bills and flipped them to the dancer. Guy took a dollar from the change the hostess had left, crumpled it into a ball and tossed it on stage. He watched the dancer pick up the others' money, then finally his offering, feeling a sense of connection with her. He finished his beer, then looked around for the hostess to order another.

There was an argument in the back between two hostesses. None of the other customers were aware of it because of the clapping and cheering of the crowd while the dancer gathered her cast-off clothes and, using them marginally to cover her nakedness, glissaded off the stage. A Korean bouncer had intervened, grabbing one of the hostesses by the arm and forcing her through a back door. Guy noticed that it was his hostess.

He got the attention of another hostess, a Vietnamese woman, who took his order. He waited. The volume of the music from the jukebox was turned up a couple of notches. Then another Korean hostess with a rushed look on her face brought his beer, right before the next performance.

This dancer was hapa—she looked local—and was not as tall and as openly sexual in her movements as the first dancer, but her beauty seemed purer. There was a light tan to her skin, and when she took off her top, her true cream color became obvious. She didn't smile, her face holding a somberness and her eyes a kind of airiness. It was difficult to tell if she was liking what she was doing or not.

Guy stared at her profile, and, as if feeling his eyes on her, she returned the stare. He tried to hold their exchange, but he backed off, taking his beer and sipping it. When he looked up, her back was facing him. He sipped his beer again.

I'm gonna get drunk, he told himself. Maybe I'll go and talk to her afterwards, backstage.

Yes, the beer would make him bolder. He'd drink on so that he could make his move. He had to make a move. Perhaps tonight was the night. He was going to be thirty-six and had nothing to show. Maybe she is the one. He needed a wife, at least a girlfriend, and this girl would be perfect. He fantasized sleeping with her. And he wondered how their children would look, she being hapa and her beauty transferring to their children. They would be beautiful children. Everyone would comment how adorable they looked.

She was lying on stage, legs spread and half-shut eyes rolling. He took in the fantasy.

By the end of the third performance, Guy was drunk and feeling bold. During the third show, he had locked eyes with the dancer and didn't look away. Even with the hostess he was suggestive, patting her on the rump and asking her to sit with him. She returned during the intermission to pour the rest of his beer.

"Whas yo' name?" he asked.

Tiffany, she said. "You wanna buy Tiffany champagne?"

"How much?"

"Oh, why you ask how much? You like Tiffany come sit with you, you buy Tiffany champagne."

So Guy bought her champagne. She took Guy to a booth in the back of the lounge where it was darker, and two other hostesses joined them. The bottle was a little larger than a bottle of beer, and the champagne went fast. They ordered a second bottle and a third, all going down quickly. Guy had enough time to make the initial small talk before the girls left him (he didn't even get a feel); there was no money for a fourth bottle.

The three bottles of champagne had cost him thirty dollars apiece. He ended up drinking two more beers in the booth by himself until last call was given. Staggering out of the booth, he thought of finding the hapa dancer. But the Korean man who had taken the first hostess off the floor told him at the back door that Phoebe had long gone home. He was going to ask about the second hostess, but he saw her walking out with someone else. He left the lounge.

Outside, he stood under the bright neon sign of the bar, looking up at it. Then the sign went off. That's the way of my life, he thought, the lights go on and then off. Pfff. He got into his car and sat for a few minutes with his hands resting on the steering wheel. He was hungry but broke. At two-thirty in the morning the only option was to go home and sleep it off, maybe get charged up by a Penthouse or Playboy before crashing. But it was a nice early morning, and the stars were crisp and the moon full. He decided to take a drive down the freeway, to where the freeway ended, then go back home to Kānewai.

There were the usual Friday night cars on the freeway, joyriding at seventy-plus in their speed machines, though there were fewer of them as Guy approached the end of the freeway. He enjoyed the ride, with the windows down and the cool wind chilling him and the radio blasting old sixties rock and roll tunes that he thought he had forgotten the words of but didn't.

On the shoulder of the freeway about a mile before it ended, Guy spotted a parked vehicle with its hood up. At first he wasn't going to stop, but something—the moon, perhaps, or the stars—suddenly made him. He braked fast and came to a stop behind the car, keeping the car and lights running. The stalled vehicle was old, and it bothered him that he could not figure out what kind of car it was, for he always took pride that he could discern the make, type and year of any American or Japanese car. A short old man appeared from the front of the car, shielding his eyes from the bright headlights. Guy took a flashlight from the glove compartment and got out.

"You need some help?"

The old man smiled. "I dunno whas wrong wit' my car. Nevah give me problems befo'."

"What happened?"

"I dunno. I was driving when da buggah jus' wen ma-ke on me. Everyt'ing wen go. Da lights wen pio. Everyt'ing. Lucky thing nevah had no cars on da road."

"Try let me look."

Guy poked his flashlight into the engine compartment. He checked for leaks or unusual smells. There were none. He inspected the hoses and wires, looking for a loose connection. He opened the air cleaner and examined it.

"You sure you get 'nuff gas?"

"Oh, yeah. I jus' wen fill up not too long ago. Tonight, in fact."

"Try start 'em."

The old man got in and tried to start the car. The starter engaged, but the engine wouldn't kick. He told the old man to stop. Guy checked the dipstick. There was enough oil, no burning smell either. Then he found a loose main lead from the distributor. He cleaned the contact points and replugged the wire, sure that he had found the problem. And the car started.

The old man was unending in his thanks to Guy. "Eh, you saved my life, son. Here." And he gave Guy a rag to wipe his hands. The old man reached into his back pocket for his wallet and took out a bill. "Here," the old man said, "fo' yo' trouble."

Guy thought the night was playing tricks with his eyes. But that was the $100 president on the bill. His hand moved unsurely towards the money, but he pulled it back. "Nah," he said, waving his refusal. "Nah."

"Go take yo' girlfriend out, have a good time."

Guy shrugged his shoulders. "Nah, das all right. I no need da money."

"No, I want you take it. Here." The old man folded the bill and tried to slip it in Guy's shirt pocket.

Guy stepped away, covering the pocket.

"Why you no like take my thank you? My money stay dirty or what? You no like take yo' girlfriend out?"

"Nah, is not dat."

The old man regarded Guy strangely. "Eh, I not poor. I can afford this. Here . . . take dah money."

"Nah, das all right."

"No-no. Das not *all right*. You help me, so I give you dis . . . from my heart. Here . . . take 'em. You and yo' girlfriend. Go holoholo someplace."

Guy shrugged his shoulders. "Nah, das okay. I get money. And anyway . . . I no mo' one girlfriend."

"Oh . . . okay. So you no' mo' one girlfriend go spend money on. Ah . . . now I see dah problem."

Guy gave back the rag. "You all right den, eh? Yo' car?" He started walking back to his car.

"Wait a minute." The old man chased after Guy and gave

him a business card. "Try check dis place out. I think you going
find just what you want at dis place."

"Whas dis?" Guy read the card in the illumination of his
headlights:

Angels

A COMPLETE ESCORT SERVICE

*Choose from Our Unique Selection
of Beautiful Paradisaic Women*

Your Satisfaction Is Guaranteed!

MAJOR CARDS WELCOMED! NO CHECKS PLEASE!

CALL 4AN-GELS

"Jus' call up," the old man advised, "and tell dem Joseph told
you about dis place. Dey going geev you one complimentary
pass."

"What is dis place? One massage parlor?"

The old man grinned. "A place where you going find yo'
one and only, *true* angel."

"Dis is one escort service, eh? But you gotta pay. I did dis
one time and dey wen soak me."

"No worry. You mention my name and dey going geev you
one complimentary pass. Is not what you think." Then the old
man waved him away.

Guy slipped the card into his wallet and returned to his car.
Moments later he was a quarter of a mile down the freeway.
He peeked into the rearview mirror and saw the headlights of
the old man's car switch on. At the end of the freeway, he
glimpsed into the mirror again, but now there was no trace
of the car. Maybe the old man's car is stalled again, he thought,
but let someone else help him. He exited the freeway and made
a U-turn to get back on, heading in the opposite direction.
Strange, he thought, as he looked over to the other side of the

freeway at the site of the breakdown. He could not find a sign of the old man's car.

Saturday night was spent watching television and half-listening to the rambling comments of his mother. He turned in early. Sunday was uneventful, but when was a day eventful for Guy Matsuzaki? The following work week dragged on, with Naka getting more and more irritable. Almost anything Guy did was reason for a complaint. He thought seriously of quitting for the first time in seventeen years, but he knew that he just couldn't do it. He had never worked anywhere else and was afraid to even think of looking for another job. What kept him going through the week were fantasies about the hapa dancer and the Korean hostess.

Friday night was another night at Paradise Lounge. The same girls were dancing, but without the hapa one. He hoped that the good-looking Korean hostess would be there, but she too was not there. This time he did not get into the champagne trap and left the lounge early, feeling something was not quite right with himself. Sitting low in the driver's seat of his car in the lounge's parking lot, he again envied his married friends and imagined what it would be like to have a woman whom he could come home to. He had never experienced romance before. He never had a way with women, always in love with one but never able to get her to feel the same way about him. He was short and skinny. Throw in stupid, too. Girls never care for guys with no sex appeal. It didn't matter that he was a good worker and had never been late at the shop. If for one night he could be a Marlboro man, he would give up anything.

He started up the car and left the lot. He could not bear to watch two people holding hands and kissing so wantonly out in the open like that couple was doing at the back entrance. Driving along a row of bars, he glanced up at the sky, wanting to see some stars, but the bar signs were just too bright, erasing their existence. Perhaps he could go to a park away from all of this, he told himself, sit on a bench and watch the glistening of the stars. Better than going home and watching television with his mother.

Then he thought about the card that the old man had given him. Several times during the past week he had taken it out of his wallet and looked it over, then slipped it back in, each time telling himself how foolish he would be if he called the number. But now, with several beers loosening his thinking, he thought that calling the number was perhaps not a bad idea.

He spotted a pay phone in front of a darkened floral shop. He got out, dropped in a quarter and dialed the number. A woman answered, and when he mentioned Joseph, there was a pause, followed by a lowering of the woman's voice. Directions to the establishment followed.

It took him about twenty minutes to get to the highrise, which was located in a good section of town. At the front door Guy punched in the code the woman had given him. He caught the elevator to the twenty-third floor, found the apartment and rang the doorbell. The door opened by itself, and Guy cautiously entered a small bright room that was singly furnished with a folding metal chair. A closed window and a handleless door were set in one wall; on another wall hung a lithograph of an old painting, a nude white woman standing in a clam shell, surrounded by other nudes and cherubs. Guy was drawn to the painting, in particular the large breasts and wide thighs of the central figure.

The window slid open.

"Mr. Matsuzaki?" A young local woman was on the other

side. She had short brown hair and was slender and pretty. Her eyes were freshly made up, and she had on a sky-blue sleeveless gown.

"Yes?" But how did she know his name?

"I'm sorry to keep you waiting for so long."

"No . . . I jus' got here."

"Mr. Gabriel told us about you and asked that we provide you with our best service. Thank you for coming to Angels."

"Mr. Gabriel?"

"Oh." She blushed. "I mean Joseph. We call him Mr. Gabriel. Anyway, Mr. Gabriel informed us that you are looking for a wife. Is this information correct?"

Guy was stunned. Embarrassed, despite being drunk.

"Is the information correct, Mr. Matsuzaki?"

He couldn't answer the woman who was smiling sweetly at him.

"Mr. Matsuzaki, are you feeling all right? Can I get you something?"

"Yeah . . . I mean, yes, I am. Yes, I guess I am."

"You are . . . ?"

He looked away from the woman's scrutiny. "I guess . . . I am looking for one," he said, his eyes lowering.

"For a wife?"

"Uh . . . yeah. Yes."

"Very well. Please come in."

The door slid open. He stood there, undecided.

"Please come in," the woman persuaded with a smile.

Guy stepped into a small inner room where she took his hand and shook it—her hand was cold . . . perhaps because of the air-conditioning?—and introduced herself as Thalia, then led him down a short corridor that led to another door that opened into a large white room. Thalia stopped before entering the room and motioned Guy to go ahead. "I hope you have an enjoyable experience here," she said, closing the door partly. The room contained a red leather sofa and a black coffee table. On the table was a white folder.

"Please sit down, Mr. Matsuzaki. Someone will be right with you. Meanwhile, please refer to our file of angels. Thank you."

She closed the door.

Guy scanned the room. The walls were bare, and there was another knobless door on the opposite wall. He sat on the cold sofa, but it was too soft, and he had to sit balanced on the edge of the seat to prevent himself from sinking in. He opened the folder to the first page:

Welcome to *THE HOUSE OF ANGELS.*

We are a complete escort service that will provide you with THE BEST OF MANY WORLDS. We mean to give you supreme satisfaction or we will promptly refund YOUR ORIGINAL SENSE OF DESTINY.

Please view our selection of ANGELS especially chosen for *you.* HOWEVER, IF YOU DO NOT WISH TO PROCEED, PLEASE CLOSE THIS BOOK IMMEDIATELY.

After you have made your choice, please close the book, placing it back in its original position.

A guardian shortly will arrive to help you.

Thank you for choosing *THE HOUSE OF ANGELS.* We hope that your ANGEL will bring you PARADISE for more than a lifetime.

Guy browsed through the introductory instructions and turned to the next page, which contained three black-and-white photos. The photo in the lower left of the page caught his attention first. It was a nude Oriental woman lying on her side, looking off to the right of the camera. Her body was slender and her long, straight hair fell over her breasts. A small pillow hid her pudendum. His eyes followed the length of her body, lingered on what was behind the pillow, then traveled to her breasts and face. He studied the photo above the nude, which was a formal headshot of the same woman. She was perhaps in her middle or late twenties. There was something familiar about her. He scanned the next photo, a full-length shot of her in an evening dress, then returned to the nude.

He turned the page to view the next woman, and his eyes widened with recognition. Captured in the same poses as the first woman was the hapa dancer. It had to be her, he said to himself, noting the two-tone tan of her body. He continued to the next page and again was astonished: The good-looking Korean hostess was photographed in the same positions.

It was uncanny. He closed and opened his eyes. But there was no mistake. Those fingers and that ring were the hostess's. There was no mistake.

He flipped back to the first set of photographs, seized with the feeling that he had to know the woman. Then it came to him: the schoolteacher whose car he had fixed the week before. The fuel pump. The boyfriend with the shiny red sports car. But what the hell was she doing working in a place like this?

He shut the book. Was he in a dream?

He opened the book again and studied the pictures of the schoolteacher. Yes, it was her. He searched past the other photographs and found the pages blank. He was in a dream, he told himself. Or a nightmare.

It scared him. He pushed the folder away. But before he could get off the sofa, the inner door opened and a little girl with a dark complexion entered the room. She closed the door behind and, without acknowledging him, crossed the room to check if the door that Guy had come through was closed. She wore a white dress, and her long curly hair spread over her shoulders like a fan. Then she turned to Guy and smiled, her cheeks each embellished with a dimple.

"Hi. My name is Leilani," she said, standing in front of him. "My name means 'Wreath of Heaven.'" She smiled again, making her dimples more prominent. "Can I help you now?"

"Yeah. How you get out of here?"

The girl giggled. "Oh no, Mr. Matsuzaki! Don't be afraid. I know it's strange, but Mr. Gabriel is a real nice man. He just wants to help you. Please come with me." She reached over to take his hand.

"No," he said, withdrawing his hand from hers. "I don't wanna stay here. I wanna get out of here. This is one strange place. I wish I nevah take this trip."

"Trip?"

"Yeah, one trip. Jus' like I'm on drugs."

"Oh, I guess you could call it a trip. But come, Mr. Matsuzaki, please come. Don't be afraid." The girl's singsong voice was pleasant, but still Guy resisted.

"No, I like get out of here. Show me how I can get out."

"Please come with me. Mr. Gabriel wants you to enjoy yourself."

"Where you going take me?"

The girl looked at the door and back. "I'm going to take you to Miss Yokota."

"Who?"

"Miss Yokota. Your first selection."

"What first selection?"

"Didn't you choose Miss Yokota?"

"Who's dat?"

"Miss Yokota, the first selection in the book."

"What do you mean I chose her?"

"Isn't she your first choice?"

Guy took in a breath, flipped to the photos, then returned to the girl's waiting smile.

"No . . . I no want her."

"Then how about Miss Kimberly."

"Which one is that?"

The girl grinned. "Oh, Mr. Matsuzaki, you're funny!"

The hapa girl, Guy thought.

"And what's the name of the last girl?"

"You mean Miss Lim? Oh, she's very pretty. And she's very nice. But Miss Kimberly is also very pretty and very nice. And so is Miss Yokota. Come, Mr. Matsuzaki. She's waiting."

"Who's waiting?"

"Miss Yokota."

"I said I don't want her. I want—I want—"

The girl folded her arms over her chest, tapping one foot impatiently.

"Uh, how about . . . the second one. Kimberly. Miss Kimberly."

A smile burst forth from the girl. "Oh, she's so perfect! She's a very good choice. Come, Mr. Matsuzaki, and let's meet her!"

"But wait—"

"No waits, Mr. Matsuzaki. Miss Kimberly is *dying* to see you."

"She's waiting . . . back there?"

She nodded her head and took his hand. Guy gave small resistance, but got up and let the girl lead him through the inner door.

"She knows I'm coming?"

"Why of course, Mr. Matsuzaki! You're so funny!"

"But what about Miss Yokota? Isn't she waiting too?"

"Oh, Mr. Matsuzaki! You're so funny! Come. Let's go."

He followed her down a metal staircase, their hollow foot-steps echoing beneath them. A naked light bulb at each turn weakly illuminated the steps. Guy heard the door close above them.

"Where you taking me now?"

She stopped. "You're going to meet Miss Kimberly. Remem-ber? Oh, Mr. Matsuzaki, you're so funny!"

Guy almost smiled. The little girl was relaxing him. But he caught himself. Kids were known to be drug runners. What if the girl was setting him up to be mugged? He glanced over his shoulder.

At the bottom of the staircase was a large metal door with a handle bar. The girl stopped and let go of his hand.

"Bye, Mr. Matsuzaki. I hope you have a really nice life with Miss Kimberly. She's super nice and super beautiful. Good-bye." The little girl waved and started up the staircase.

"Hey, wait! What—what you doing? Where—what—am I supposed to do?"

The girl continued up the stairs, pointed at the door with a jabbing motion, then waved again, disappearing around a turn in the stairway.

"Hey!" He ran up after her, but she had disappeared. "Christ! What da hell is going on?" A chill grabbed him in the gut. He retreated, slowly climbing down the stairs.

Cautiously he pushed through the metal door and found himself outside of the building. The air was fresh and cool. He shook his head, letting go of the door, which closed qui-etly behind him. Maybe as a prank someone at the bar had slipped a hallucinogen in his drink. Was he experiencing an acid trip? Had he been taken for a fool . . . again? He tottered back and peered up at the building's dizzying height. The stars were above, bright and twinkling. He checked his watch. It was eleven-thirty-three. Only three minutes had passed? He tapped his watch with disbelief.

Then a panic came over him.

He raced down the street to his car, got in and started it with a roar. Running two traffic lights, he entered the freeway where he pressed the accelerator to eighty.

He failed to see an easy turn in the freeway. The car clipped the guardrail, then fishtailed and spun three times around before slamming into a concrete piling.

Once upon a time there lived a mechanic by the name of Guy Matsuzaki. He was a hard worker and a nice man. But he was a lonely man, for never in his life did he have steady female companionship, and now that he was reaching his thirty-sixth birthday, he wanted more than anything else the company of a wife.

One day, after a long day at the shop, he decided to go out and have a drink. He drove to an area of the city where many hostess bars were known to be located. Perhaps I will find my mate tonight, he said to himself. He read the sign of one lounge—Angel Lounge—and the name attracted him. So he parked his car in front of the establishment. Entering the front door, he instantly found many beautiful women inside, laughing and talking and drinking and dancing with each other. But he was too shy to approach any of them. It pained him to think about his numerous past rejections by women. He sat on a barstool and ordered a beer and, using the mirror mounted behind the bar, watched the beautiful women enjoying each other's company.

An old man two barstools down from him was watching Guy

with interest. "So you're a man in want," the stranger began. Guy pretended not to hear him. The old man's voice was familiar, but Guy could not place it. "Never mind," the old man said. "You no hav' to answer me. I know why you come here. You one lonely man, jus' like all dese other guys here." And the old man turned to the other men sitting at the bar whom Guy had not noticed when entering the lounge. "You come to the right place, son. But look at dese other guys. Dey losers." The old man laughed. "And you know why dey losers?" Guy wasn't looking at the old man, but he was listening. "'Cause you came in. 'Cause you da one I was waiting fo'!"

Guy turned to the old man. "Who you?"

The old man shook his head. "You no remember? You no remember you wen help me one time on the freeway?" He laughed. "Nevah mind. No matter." And he moved over to the stool next to Guy's. "I going tell you something," he whispered. "You see all dose girls over dere? Come closing time all of dem going disappear through dat door." He pointed to a narrow doorway in the back of the lounge that was covered by strings of colorful plastic beads. "Dey going in there and disappear." He smiled. "You see," he whispered, glancing around to see that no one else was listening, "dey go back there to put on dey wings. And den dey going fly back to da heavens. Das where dey all come from. Dey angels. Dey come down here fo' have one good time. But come closing time, dey gotta go back home. Das why dey call dis place Angel Lounge. Make sense, no?" The old man chuckled.

Guy still could not place the man's voice or face. "I know you from someplace, but I cannot remember."

"You lonely, right? You want one wife?"

Guy regarded the old man curiously. "What you talking about?"

"I tell you what fo' do."

"Wait—wait. Why you telling me all dis?"

"Nevah mind. I know why you came inside here. No worry. I know." And he whispered into Guy's ear.

Guy resisted. "Why you telling me this?"

"Eh, no play games with me. All right?"

All Guy could do was nod his head. The old man repeated the last part of the instructions: "But remember: Wait until you get four children. Or else you going be like dese losers sitting around here. Dey lost dey chance already. Dey going spend da rest of dey time sitting around here and drinking and looking in da mirror. You, only, get one chance. If you no like come back like dese sorry cases, remember what I said." Then he coaxed Guy off the stool with a nudge of his elbow.

Twenty minutes later, Guy came back to the barstool with a worried look on his face. He chugged down what was left of his warm beer.

"You did what I tol' you fo' do?" the old man asked.

Guy nodded his head. He was perspiring.

"Good. Then you get nothing fo' worry about. Jus' remember what I tol' you: Wait 'til you get four children."

Guy nodded his head, then ordered another beer.

"Now we jus' wait fo' closing time."

They talked little, and by the bar's last call, Guy was drunk. His head was on the bar.

"Eh, now's da time!" the old man cried, shaking Guy hard. "Now's da time. Get up! She stay waiting fo' you outside!"

Guy straightened up. Rubbing his eyes, he turned to an empty dance floor. Bright lights had been turned on. Everything was making him dizzy.

"You bettah get yo' ass out there. Pronto!"

"She waiting . . . outside?"

"Yes, jus' like I tol' you. Hurry up befo' you lose yo' chance and some other buggah grab her."

Guy shot out the back exit and into the empty parking lot. And there he found a wingless, weeping angel sitting on a stool. He approached her warily, finally asking her if she needed help. She looked up and said no, wiping the tears from her eyes. He asked if there was anything wrong. She said that her ride was late. He told her that he could give her a ride if she wanted, or wait with her. She said okay to the wait, that she wouldn't mind having some company. And they began to talk. He found out that her name was Kimberly, but somehow, strangely, he had already known that her name was Kimberly. And they talked until the sky began to lighten. Guy asked her again if she needed a ride home, and she said, with a choke in her voice, that she had no home, that she had just moved . . . no, that she was actually between moves. And he offered to let her stay for the day at his apartment. And without hesitation, she thanked him and said all right. And they went to his apartment, and she never left.

They were married shortly after, and a few months later they were parents to a beautiful daughter. And a year later, a handsome son. Another year and another lovely daughter. And their days together were wonderful and happy and full of love and warmth.

One day Guy came home after a long hard day at work, sat at the kitchen table and drank his usual couple of beers to relax. As usual, too, he counted the blessings of his life. But instead of stopping after two beers, as he customarily did, he continued to drink until he was rather drunk. His wife sat next to him, clearly saddened.

"Something wrong wit' you?" he asked, concerned.

She said nothing. Guy prodded her, for he did not like secrets kept from him. Finally, she gave in.

"I had a dream last night. I dreamt of my sisters and they were crying. Husband, I am very happy here with you and the children. But I want to go back home and visit with my sisters. I sense that something is wrong there. And they must be very worried about me, too. Do you . . . have any idea where my wings are?"

The request stunned him. She had never asked him about her wings. He shook his head, took a long swig of beer, and avoided her watchful eyes. Yes, of course he knew where her wings were, he could not deny the truth. But perhaps if he did not answer at all, this would not count as lying, as he cherished their relationship, which was from the start one of honesty and trust. She asked the question again, and again, and finally, unable to resist further because of his drunken state of mind, he succumbed to her soft pleadings.

"Yes, yes," he conceded. "I know where your wings are."

"Oh please, tell me where they are! Please! I have never asked you this before, but now, after this terrible dream, I must go and visit my sisters. Please!"

He told her that the wings were hidden in the garage, inside a yellow tool box. She disappeared to the garage, leaving Guy with a growing troubled feeling. She returned with the wings, which were neatly folded into a small bundle, and brushed off the dust that had settled on them all those years. She caressed and fondled them as if they were a newborn baby. She held them to her face, closed her eyes and began singing a song that Guy had never heard before. He could not understand the words. The melody was heavy and repetitive, reminding him of the ebb and flow of waves on a shore.

Before Guy could say a word, Kimberly slipped into the wings and called for the children. "I must go back." Her voice had deepened. "You have been a wonderful husband, a wonderful companion to me. But I must return to my sisters."

And when the children had gathered, she led them out of the house.

Guy ran after them: "Where are you going? Don't leave! Don't leave!"

Under a full moon partly hidden by clouds, Kimberly and the children began to glow with a yellow aura as the wings expanded dreadfully. It scared Guy. He could not move or say a word, paralyzed by that terrible vision. Kimberly lowered her wings and turned to him, her face long and pale, and their eyes met in a cold and distant recognition. Then she helped the oldest child climb on her back and held one clinging child in each arm. Spreading her wings again, which had grown long and thick, then flapping them gracefully, then faster, then violently, she rose off the ground, the obedient expressionless children clutching their mother, and disappeared into the clouds.

With tears rolling down brokenly on his cheeks, his body shaking and his eyes lost in the fierce stirring in the clouds, he wailed and begged to the heavens, and choked on the vomit of his drunkenness.

THE GUEST

At first, Colbert Nakamatsu wasn't worried that his friend from high school, Herman Penorio, Jr., whom Colbert hadn't spoken to since the day they both departed their separate ways to boot camp twenty-three years ago, was encamped in his front yard, under the fruit-burdened mango tree. In the kitchen Colbert had said to his wife that he didn't mind Herman staying there, that his friend wasn't going to cause any trouble "cuz I know him from grade school time." A few days earlier, coming from his job as an apprentice pipefitter at the Pearl Harbor Naval Shipyard, Colbert was about to turn up his driveway when he noticed mango pits and peeled skins scattered all over the road. That's when he saw Herman sitting on the exposed root of a tree, sucking on the butt of a cigarette, holding it as if it were a marijuana roach. Colbert pretended that he didn't see him and continued up to the house.

"But what if he stay?" Susan Nakamatsu grumbled. "Then what you going do?"

Away from the complaining of his supervisor, Colbert felt

the need to relax. He took two bottles of beer from the refrigerator, opened one with a hard twist, and guzzled down a third of the contents as he swaggered to the living room, his broad frame brushing against the door jamb. "He not," he said calmly to his wife before belching.

"How you know, Mister Always-with-one-answer?"

"Cuz I know," he said as he lazed into his worn armchair. He quaffed down another third. "Cuz I know him from grade school time."

"You always say that. 'Cuz I know him from grade school time.' As if that the secret to everything."

"Just about." Colbert finished the beer and opened the other. Two was his usual limit, but today, especially with Susan in her picky mood, perhaps three might get him through the early evening without losing his temper.

"You know, his bruddah one real pain-in-dah-butt. Always talking 'bout Hawaiian dis, Hawaiian dat. Next thing you know, he going claim half of Kānewai as dah Hawaiian kingdom, with him as king."

"Who? Herman? Eh . . . where dah remote?"

"I wasn't talking about Herman, but maybe him, too. Maybe he listening to what all his bruddah saying. You don't know."

"And *you* don't know. Herman . . . he not going do that. He too . . . too . . . "

"There you go, protecting your friend. And you guys not even friends. Since when dah last time you associated with him? Twenty years?"

Colbert found the remote right in front of him, on the coffee table, half-tucked under a disarray of the week's newspapers. He powered up the TV. "Twenty-three. Eh, don't get on his case. He fought fo' his country, and maybe his mind not all there, but at least respect dah guy fo' what he is."

"But—"

"I said shut up!"

Colbert glared towards the kitchen, towards his wife who was hidden behind the refrigerator. He heard Susan throw something metallic into the sink. Then he switched the channel to ESPN.

From a short distance, Herman looked like, according to Susan, "one alien from one science fiction movie." He was tall, over six feet, and thin. He had not cut his hair since he shaved his head, which was five years after he joined the Marine Corps and eight months and twenty-two days after he entered the VA psychiatric ward in San Francisco. His hair had grown long and matted, down the length of his back, like a thick, wooly brown carpet with its fibers bunching up. His beard was thin and long, dangling to just above where his piko would be. And he always was dressed in brown, or rather, anything he wore eventually turned to the color of the ground.

The children at the nearby elementary school had nick-named him Guava Man. In the thicket behind the gas tank of the cafeteria, Herman had, for a period of two months at the start of one school year, found himself a home. There was a lot of guava and lilikoi for the picking, and running water was available from the school's various drinking fountains. But this quest of Herman for a sedentary life ended when one of the parents, an off-duty police officer, became enraged at Herman's blatant display of perversion that was viewed by a line of kindergarteners waiting along the concrete walkway to enter the cafeteria. At home, Ku'uipo Perreira had said to her father, "Daddy, I saw Guava Man's ding-ding." Actually, Herman had been just taking a piss, next to the gas tank. There was no twisted bone anywhere in Herman's body, but tell that to Lance Perreira and he'd tell you where to go. Stomping into the thicket, off-duty officer Perreira ordered his second cousin on his mother's side to beat it or "I going beat dah shit outta you—you—you goddamn fucking pervert!" Knowing better than to tangle with a 223–pound heifer, Herman dug out the back way of the thicket, never to return.

It was about the seventh day of Herman's occupation of Colbert's front yard that Colbert began to be bothered by the look-the-other-way demeanor of his former friend. Upon coming home from work that day, Colbert discovered a faded but true-colored Hawaiian flag suspended between two lower branches of the mango tree. (Herman had discovered the flag improperly disposed of in the school's garbage bin and had used it, until its present new purpose, as a towel, pillow or blanket.) Herman's sleeping under *his* mango tree and eating *his* fruit and casting the remains onto *his* street were things that Colbert could handle. But showing the colors—even if they were faded—of the Hawaiian flag on his property . . . that was something else. Still, Colbert decided to remain silent, despite the prodding occasional "You see" from his wife.

One morning, before taking off for work, Colbert made an effort to offer a styrofoam cup of freshly brewed coffee to his former friend, but repeated callings could not stir a snoring Herman from his loft on a lower limb of the tree.

"You gotta do something, Colbert." Susan was washing the dinner dishes and staring out the kitchen window. "Who knows. Maybe he planting pakalōlō."

She was referring to Herman's new interest, gardening. Borrowing a hoe from Colbert's garage (he didn't ask), Herman had cleared thick weeds from a patch of ground near the mango tree and furrowed five short rows for sowing.

"He planting his dream," Colbert said.

Susan stopped washing and turned to him. "He what?"

"He planting his dream."

"What you mean by that?"

"You no dream?" he said irritably. "What . . . you no dream?"

"I dream, but what that got to do with him *digging up* the ground ousside?"

"Get lot to do with it."

"Like what?"

"He like plant something. He dunno what. So right now he dreaming of what he going plant. Das all. What you think I was talking about?"

"I dunno." She shook her head slowly, returning to the dishes. "Never sound like that," she mumbled. "Just like you was saying something else."

Nobody knew what Herman had planted. Nine-year-old Denise Chang saw him throwing in one of the furrows a handful of what looked like dust. She had stopped her bicycle at the bottom of the driveway. The Nakamatsu driveway climbed a steep incline before leveling off to a flat area where the house was situated. Thick ti plants and a towering lichee tree flanked the broken macadam road. She finally got to the top of the driveway, dropped her bicycle on the overgrown crab grass and entered the house, calling, "Trisha! Trisha! Come see what Guava Man doing!"

Trisha Nakamatsu, playing with her Lego set in her room, heard her school friend calling and scampered out to the parlor. "What you wen say?"

"Guava Man. He t'rowing dirt in dah dirt."

"What?"

"Guava Man, he planting dirt."

"Whachu mean?"

So Denise had to explain, with as much detail as she could, exactly what she had seen.

"Hi, Denise," Susan said, coming in from the back where she had just collected the laundry from the clotheslines. "Whachu was saying about Guava Man?"

"He trying grow dirt."

"You can say that again." Susan made a sour face, thinking about the years of filth caked on Herman's body. "He should take one good bath, but not at my house."

"Yeah, he should grow himself," Denise said.

Susan passed by the two girls, who were now playing their patty cake greeting, trying to understand the comment of the nine-year-old.

Colbert decided not to bother Herman and to let him find his peace on that lower patch of his property. As long he stayed out of sight from the front picture window of the house, Colbert didn't mind, even with the Hawaiian flag flying, or so he told himself, though he was reminded on a daily basis of Herman's presence by his wife's near constant admonishments.

Colbert knew that Herman had gone through a whole lot. In Vietnam he had been the only survivor of a platoon that was ambushed, leaving him with two digits missing from his right hand and part of his right ear sliced off (although no one could see it now, the partial ear covered by his hair). While the Viet Cong were probing the broken bodies with the tips of their rifles, Herman had pretended to be dead. The backup platoon came three hours later, when he was semi-conscious. He had lost a lot of blood, but they did get him out and eventually back to the states, where he recovered at a VA hospital. Though he lived months of a stunned existence there, doctors finally diagnosed that he had gotten back his mind. But back home, stoned out of his head on reds, pakalōlō and booze in a backyard barbeque at Waimalu Housing, he flipped out after the four-year-old daughter of his friend Jason said to him, "Uncle Hermie, smurf like talk to you." And the smurf did start talking to him, rambling on and on about how he was sick and tired of being dragged here and there by a little girl, of being used as a kleenex for tears and snot, of being slept on and stepped on, and of being thrown into the washing machine and tossed and pulled apart. Frightened by this angry blue being, Herman's soul leaped out of his body. Herman— rather, the body— crumpled to the ground. "Eh . . . Hermie? You all right?" his friend asked, then started laughing, thinking it funny that an adult would be frightened by a stuffed doll. The others began laughing. Someone joked that perhaps the Kona Gold was too strong for Herman to handle.

Herman slowly got up. He had no words to say to anyone, facility with words having left him, too. He brushed off the pakalōlō ash from his t-shirt and bits of dead grass on the seat of his pants, then walked away, never speaking a word to anyone for seventeen years.

"You read dis morning's newspepah?" Sheila Sample said to her husband, Manō.

The neighbor across the street from the Nakamatsus dropped slices of bread into the toaster. Manō sat at the table and shook out a fold in the newspaper. "I reading it now," he said.

"Terrible. About Abraham Penorio."

"Who's dat?"

"Abraham Penorio? Das dah Herman across-dah-street's bruddah."

Manō sipped his coffee and with his eyes nudged her to go on.

"Terrible," she continued. "I mean, I Hawaiian, and I proud of being one Hawaiian. But this kine Hawaiian sovereignty and what-have-you is fo' dah birds. Eh, I proud also being one American."

Manō turned to the sports pages and scanned the box scores. "So what dis hafto do wit' dah Penorio boy?"

"Dah bruddah stay 'cross dah street."

"Who?"

"Dah oldah bruddah."

"What oldah bruddah?"

"Manō, you listening to me o' what?"

"Yeah." His eyes stopped at the stats of his favorite major league pitcher.

"I said dah Penorio boy."

"Which one?"

"Dah one 'cross dah street."

"So what he got to do wit' dah kine Hawaiian sovereignty."

"Aehh! No sense talk to you. You always confusing me. I talking 'bout Abe Penorio, dah youngah bruddah of Herman's."

"Oh . . . dah radical one?"

"Yeah."

"What about him?" Manō's Yankees weren't doing well, losing to the Indians seven to one. His favorite pitcher was shelled for five runs in the second inning before being pulled out of the game.

"He no mo' shame, him. He go demonstrate dah Federal building."

"Das his right."

"What right? To make trouble? He gotta be crazy."

"Das what one American is fo'."

"What you mean?"

Chrissakes, Manō thought. The American League is going crazy. Mariners whipping the Red Sox by thirteen runs. Toronto beating the Angels by fifteen. He looked up to his wife. "What you mean, 'What I mean?'"

"'Bout being one American. Going demonstrate like one nut is not being American. Das communist, you ask me."

"We get free speech, right? So anybody can speak their piece."

"But not in one crazy kine way."

"Why? Whas so nuts hanging dah Hawaiian flag? Eh, if I had one Hawaiian flag, maybe I hang 'em too."

"What you talking 'bout? Hang what flag?"

"Dah Hawaiian flag. So whas wrong demonstrate dah Hawaiian flag? I proud be one Hawaiian."

"Das not my point."

"Den whas yo' point. Befo' you burn dah toast." He gave her another nudging look, this time for the toast that had just popped.

"I not talking 'bout that. I talking 'bout Kawika Penorio making trouble at dah federal building."

"Well, I talking 'bout hanging dah Hawaiian flag. I proud fo' be one Hawaiian. I Hawaiian. Fifty percent. And I can fly dah flag if I like."

"Manō, make sense. I not talking 'bout flying one Hawaiian flag. I talking 'bout trying make revolution, trying overthrow dah government."

Manō lowered the newspaper, his eyes narrowing with suspicion. "What you said?"

Other neighbors were asking the Nakamatsus about Herman
Penorio and especially about the tattered Hawaiian flag hanging from the tree in their front yard. And they always had to
explain that it wasn't their flag and that they hadn't hung the
flag, and the talk always led to a silence, that insinuating silence
that accused the Nakamatsus of complicity in a social crime,
a crime against the state, against the state of the mind, against
the neighborhood.

It got to the point that Colbert couldn't take it any longer.
Upon coming home from work one afternoon, he went into
the spare room and rummaged through his old clothes and
finally found, under Susan's mothballed collection of fabric
remnants, his faded fatigue jacket from his time in the service.
He changed his t-shirt, shook the jacket a few times to air it
out, then put it on. He slipped into his hunting boots and
marched down the small slope to the mango tree where he
found Herman tending his garden.

"Eh . . . Herman," Colbert started. There was a shake in his
voice. "I can talk to you?"

Herman stopped hoeing and turned to him. "Shoot. What
you like?" It was his first words for almost two decades.

Colbert was surprised to hear his former friend say anything,
but he continued as if it was business as usual. "Eh . . . like . . .
I gotta ask you fo' leave."

"Leave what?"

"Leave my house. Why you no go home?"

"I am home."

Colbert rolled his eyes. He shifted his weight from one leg

to the other. "I mean, why you no go yo' *home* home. Like yo' family's house on Henry Wilson Road."

Herman started hoeing the weeds around his foot-high ki plants. Colbert crossed his arms over his chest, shifted his weight again.

"Look," Colbert finally said, "actually I no mind you staying here on my property, but dah only problem is—"

"Dis not yo' property. Dis here, dis land, dis 'āina we standing on right now, dis is my 'āina. You wasn't using dis 'āina. I using 'em."

A small fire lit in Colbert. "What you saying? Whachu talking about?"

"I talking 'bout dis 'āina. Dis is mines one."

"Let me get dis straight wit' you. Dis is not yo' land, yo' *'āina*. You know what I mean? Dis is my land you living on. I own dis land, from here," pointing to the road, "to up deah," pointing up the slope to the house. "And if anything, you my guest, but dah way you talking to me, you not my guest. You one intruder. You know what one intruder is?" Colbert waited for an answer, which he wasn't getting. "Eh, you wanna know what—what one instruder is? I tell you what one intruder is. I want you get dah fuck outta heah, right now. Get off my property."

"You no can t'row me off dis 'āina dat you no own."

"Eh, fuck, get yo' hist'ry right."

"I know my history. *You* get dah fuck off my 'āina! You dah guest!"

Herman raised the shaft of the hoe—Colbert's hoe—to make his point, but Colbert took it as an unfriendly—rather, aggressive—gesture. He took a step backwards, noticed a blue rock on the ground and hopped to it, holding it up ready to throw. "Come on, you fuckah! You like attack me, eh? Come on, asshole. Attack."

"What you talking 'bout?" Herman realized the arbitrary way he was holding the hoe and threw the tool to the side. "Das what you like do, eh? Kill me? Den go fo' it." Herman took a few steps towards Colbert, who stumbled back. Herman squatted in front of Colbert and bent his head forward. "Go," he said with a haunting sense of sincerity, offering the back of his head. "Take one shot. Get it over with. Come on. Do it."

A cold sweat came over Colbert. He felt ridiculously stupid. He lowered the stone, then tossed it to the side. Out of frustration, he took off the jacket and threw it to the ground, then plodded back up to the house.

Colbert decided that the best way to get Herman off his land was to shut off the pipe that was supplying Herman with water. He did this on a Sunday, right after coming back from church service. By the following Wednesday, the once thriving shoots in Herman's garden were wilting. But there were no complaints from Herman, though the couple of sneak glances Colbert took while driving past the tree showed a toiling on Herman's face. Though Herman took his moisture from the juice of the mango, Colbert knew that that wasn't enough, and besides, the mango season was nearing its end. On Friday, Colbert saw Herman lying prone. He stopped the car immediately, his heart thumping with panic. Was he dead? He jumped out of the car, but before he could take another step, Herman rolled to his side, his back defiantly facing Colbert, and farted.

Colbert swore. He got back into the car and drove up the driveway. He sat in his car for a while until the trembling in his veins stopped.

In the garage closet, he took a large pipe wrench out of his toolbox and went to the side of the house to the water valve.

He opened it and, squatting, listened to the whining of the pipe wither to a quiet.

In the afternoons, after school, the mango tree became a gathering spot for some of the neighborhood children. At first, they stayed a good distance from Guava Man. The children thought that some kind of fatal disease could be caught by just breathing the air around the mango tree or by being the recipient of a look from him. But Denise Chang broke the spell one day by accident. She took a spill on her bike in front of the mango tree, her tires slipping on a rotting mango peel. Crying, blood bleeding from a gravel-scraped knee, she was suddenly in the wiry arms of Herman, who began to soothe her in quiet tones. He carried her under the mango tree and set her down on a makeshift chair made of scrap wood he had salvaged from Colbert's trash. He plucked a few leaves from one of his plants, mashed them in the palm of his hand, then pressed the poultice to the hurt. Denise stopped crying, her predicament of injury disarming her of the learned fear of Guava Man. (Upon close look, she thought Guava Man looked something like her Uncle Willy.) Herman instructed her to hold the mashed leaves in place, then went off across the lot and returned with a freshly cut ti leaf, which he fashioned into a bandage. He braided the ends together with the care of an artisan, then motioned Denise off with a wave of his hand. Without a word, the tears on her cheeks having been rubbed dry, she mounted her bike and rode off.

The next day, Denise returned and thanked Guava Man who kept with his hoeing, not even looking up once. Not getting a response, she left to see Trisha Nakamatsu. When she told Trisha about what had happened the day before, about the wound that had disappeared overnight, Trisha got curious.

Trisha called Monica Kalama on the phone and told her to meet them down on the road by the mango tree. Monica bicycled over, and the three approached Guava Man, asking about the healing powers of the plants he had growing in the previously weed-infested ground. The first thing Guava Man said to them was, "Dah weeds not weeds."

And thus began their afternoon sessions under the mango tree.

Guava Man talked to them about the different plants he had growing and the legends of the area, and when asked by the girls how did he know what kinds of plants to grow and how did he know about those stories of constellations and fish and rocks, he'd shrug his shoulders and say that he just listened to the voices that were carried by the winds. "Dey my kupuna," he said. "Dey make me understand." And in their own way, being the angels of innocence they were, the girls understood what he meant.

Trisha was, of course, aware that her parents would never allow her to go near the mango tree, so before her father would come home from work the girls would disperse, to play in another yard or house. One day, however, Colbert came home early and discovered with horror the three girls clustered around Herman. He heard Herman making them laugh, which infuriated him. Parking his car in the middle of the road, he stomped towards the gathering and, with blind rage, grabbed all three girls in his arms and carried them out from under the tree's shade, setting them down behind his car. Then he stormed back. With one hand grabbing the collar of the fatigue jacket and the other the mat of hair, he dragged Herman out on the street. Herman gave no resistance, didn't even wince in pain. The girls were horror-stricken and speechless. Colbert glowered over Herman, shaking a fist: "I no want you ever step back on my property—again!" Then he stormed back towards the mango tree and ravaged the garden and all traces of Herman's existence. And as a final measure, he tore down the Hawaiian flag, crumpled it into a ball and threw it at Herman. Ordering his daughter to get immediately to the house, he got back into his car and roared up the driveway.

But the next day Herman was back at the mango tree, the Hawaiian flag hanging from a higher branch.

Colbert was embarrassed he had acted the way he had in front of his daughter and her friends. The action he took did defuse somewhat the anger that was burning in him since the arrival of the guest, but the anger was still there. It was taking over Colbert's spirit, piercing his body with wanton urges of violence, a feeling that he had not had since thirteen years back when, at a family Christmas party, his father had scolded him for being a lazy, good-for-nothing incompetent who would never find a good job. Enraged, Colbert had thrown his massive ring of keys through the picture window of his parents' home. He ran out of the house and jumped into his Toyota Hi-Lux, but had to get out and find his set of keys among shards of glass on the hood of his father's car. Then he drove off to Waikīkī, where he got into a fight with a pack of foul-mouthed high school students.

Surprised to see Herman at the front door on a drizzly afternoon, Colbert was almost shaken with humanity to welcome his former friend into his house, just to be cordial in a "local style" kind of way, but Herman's smell—of mildew and fermented mangoes, in addition to his usual base body odor—stopped him. Before Colbert could say, "So . . . what you like," Herman, with dried saliva in the corners of his mouth,

blurted out, "You all dah t'ings you are, brah. Remembah dat."
And with that, he turned and shuffled down the steps. Colbert
put down the bag of corn chips he was eating, and he was
halfway through with a "What dah fuck you talking 'bout?"
when he choked on a half-masticated chip. By the time his
throat was cleared of the obstruction, Herman's angular gait
had disappeared behind the lower branches of the mango tree.

Colbert sat in front of the television set, trying to make sense
of what Herman had just said to him. Coughing, he went to
the kitchen and left the house through the back door. The rain
had stopped. He marched to the mango tree, approaching a
reclining Herman with the demand, "What dah hell you
come up my house and tell me dis kine bullshit? Whachu talking about anyway?"

Herman sat up and stared into Colbert's face, daring
Colbert's eyes away. "I tol' you," Herman said. "You every-
t'ing what you are, brah. And das it."

"But whachu mean by dat? Whachu trying do, fuck wit'
my mind?"

"Yo' mind already fuck up, brah. You what you are, brah.
One fat Japanee, hand fed by dah gov'ment."

"What dah fuck you talking 'bout? Who dah fuck is you
fo' talk to me like dat? I working, right? What dah fuck you
doing, fucking squattah on my fucking land! You like I call
dah cops or what?"

"You wen fuck dah land, brah. I pono-ing dah land."

"What dah hell you talkin' 'bout? Whas dis 'pono-ing'?"

"You disuse dah land. I taking care of it."

"You—you—one fucking welfare case! Get dah fuck off my
land!"

"Dis not yo' land, brah. Dis is mines."

"What?"

"Das right. You go look yo' hist'ry. Dis is Hawaiian land. You Hawaiian?"

"I—what?"

"You not Hawaiian. Dis land used to belong to my ancestors."

"I no following you. You talking crazy, man. Dis is my land. I paid for it, fair and square. But you . . . what dah fuck you ever did in yo' life that you can be proud of?"

"Eh, dis land used to belong to my ancestors. I claiming 'em back."

"Fucking crazy listening to dis. Eh, but you get one thing right. Dis *used* to be yo' ancestors land. And anyway, you not even full-bloodied Hawaiian. What you get, one fingernail Hawaiian?"

Herman rose up to his full height, which instantly sent a cautionary streak in Colbert. He hadn't realized how tall Herman was. But Colbert settled down. No matter how big he was, Colbert knew he could take him. That was a guarantee. Colbert clenched his fists, released them, then clenched them again, folding his arms across his chest, and challenged Herman with a stare.

"What you going do, fuckah?" Colbert said. "What . . . you like beef right heah?"

Herman calmly regarded the fire in Colbert's eyes. He nodded his head once, then twice, then said, "I tol' you already, brah. You all dah t'ings you are, brah. And das it. Take it or leave it."

Colbert lowered his arms, then raised his open hands in frustration. "What dah fuck you talking about? You like beef or what?"

"I said my peace. You heard me. And das it."

Herman lay on his bed of cardboard and rags.

"Eh, I like get dis all settled right here and now. I telling you again. Get off my property or I going call dah cops. You heard me?"

Herman closed his eyes and folded his hands on his chest. "Eh, I tol' you already. Get off my land. No bothah me already. Hele aku 'oe."

Colbert jumped on Herman, choked him, then punched his head over and over again, his frustrations fueling his fists. Herman raised his thin arms for protection but could not stop Colbert's rage. Colbert pulled him by his hair and dragged him to the ground, kicking him all over. Herman coiled into a ball. He again grabbed the hair and pulled the dead weight of Herman's body into the road and continued his attack.

Like a dying crayfish, Herman's body began to uncoil. Colbert stopped his kicking. Rolling on his back, Herman gasped for breath. Colbert watched, his fists numb from impact. Herman began shaking. He turned to his side and spat out blood.

"You—muddah—fock—" Herman sputtered.

"You fuckah—you like mo' lickins or what?"

"*You*—dah one—getting—dah *lickins*." Blood was coughed up.

"Hah?" Colbert's eyes narrowed on the Hawaiian flag. "Oh yeah? I tell you what. Watch dis."

Colbert threw a stone at the flag, which was now hanging from a higher branch. The rock missed its target. He threw another that hit home, though not knocking if from its perch.

It was beginning to rain again.

Colbert ran up the driveway and came back down with the mango picker from the garage. Wrapping a part of the flag around the tip of the pole, he yanked it down, then stomped it in a small puddle of mud. He tried to burn the flag with a cigarette lighter but was unsuccessful, so he ran up the driveway again and this time brought down a can of kerosene, with which he doused the flag.

Herman turned away from Colbert. He coughed up more blood. A police car had arrived, called by Manō Sample, who had witnessed the entire debacle from his garage across the street. The officer checked on Herman, who was convulsing again, and called for an ambulance.

Tossing the can to the side, Colbert lit the flag, which burst into a clean yellow flame, and the flame ignited a trail of fluid to the can where, its contents spilling, a large fire burst upwards, singeing a lower branch. And despite the fact that the tree was covered thoroughly with pebbles of rain, the branch caught on fire. The fire quickly spread, and soon the entire tree was consumed in flames.

MY FRIEND KAMMY

I'm sitting here in what you could call one fairly clean cab, under the swaying coconut trees, Honolulu, Hawai'i. Nah, Waikīkī. The cab company I work for shares the parking lot with this rock and roll club called The Clinic. Why they call it that I don't know, I didn't know there was such a thing as one rock 'n roll doctor. But then, there's so many things I don't know about nowadays. I'm looking at all these foxy chicks slinking into the bright neon doorway of the club, followed by packs of roving sharks. Looking for some meat, those sharks are hungry tonight. Every night they're hungry.

I wonder where Kammy is? Probably cruising the streets. Sometimes he does that for the entire night, driving round and round in circles, never stopping unless for a pickup. Crazy.

Slow night tonight. Nobody in the stand but me. Wish I never have to work tonight. Shit, but I made this agreement with the owner of the cab, that I would rent his cab for at least six nights a week. Ah well, just as well. No more nothing for me to do at home but watch the goddamn boob tube.

Goddamn owner, goddamn capitalist. Squeezing every other dollar from me.

Ahhh . . . he's a good guy. I smoke with him once in awhile. But everytime seems like I the one bringing the doobies. Christ, what a fucken tightass.

This fucking seat is real had-it. Goddamn, the fucking owner, he can paint the cab real nice outside, but inside sucks. Shit, my ass almost touching the floor. And the goddamn transmission making all kinds of sounds. Well, that's not my problem. Shit, but I been getting this backache for the past three or four weeks. I bet is because of this fucking seat. Shit.

Maybe I should go to that rock 'n roll club tonight. Pick up one babe or two. Christ . . . you must be kidding yourself, eh, Bobby? Who the fuck going look at one burnt-out, Oriental hippie . . . with his hair in one ponytail and long enough to almost touch his ass? Christ, the haole girls before used to dig my hair, they used to go nuts with it. And look at me, streaks of white hair, thick wire-rimmed glasses. You think you have one chance with those young girls or what? Shit. Old man already . . . And look how they all dress nowdays, green hair fancy clothes bright colors designer shades . . . eh, what happened to owning one pair blue jeans?

God, what I would do for one joint right now. Or one good lay. I think I would have the lay over the joint. Bilot, as Kammy would say. Shit, I'm suppose to be liberal-minded, a sixties person, I'm suppose to not think male chauvinist thoughts. But right now all I want is a good fuck that I haven't had for almost nine months, some fine ass just sitting on my face. And maybe one nice joint to confuse my mind while stroking like mad.

You know, sometimes I think us cabdrivers are just as bad as the hookers on Hotel Street. Here we are, shuttling the military dumdums back and forth, base to Waikīkī or Hotel Street, Waikīkī or Hotel Street back to base, or trying to con some haole tourist into one inflated tour around the island. That kind of thing. We're just appendages to the economy, more or less. We're not a necessary element. And so are the hookers. While we hunt for that big-money ride, they're trying to sucker in some military jerk or tourist into a fifty-buck fuck. Or more. They know when to up the ante. Take for example the time I picked up this Japanese tourist on the street.

Nighttime. Corner of Kuhio and Liliʻuokalani. The guy looks my age. Looks something like a junior executive from Toyota. Or something like that. He can't speak English, so he's making this funny sign with his fingers, spreading out the middle and index and sliding his other index finger up and down between them. Can't figure out what he wants. Then he starts saying good-good or something like that, and then I figure out what he wants.

These Japanese executives, they come down here and all they want is to fuck a haole girl, perferably one blonde. So I go down Kuhio and take a left turn down Kaiulani, and just down a little bit he starts slapping the back of my seat excitedly, pointing to a tall leggy blonde in front of a gift shop. So I pull over to the side. He rolls down his window and before you know it, we're swarmed by these night ladies, poking their heads and hands in, they know when the big game fish is lurking in their waters. The fucking Japanee national, he really gets off on this. These fucking nationals, they fucking worship the haoles so bad . . . so pitifully. Like I had my share of white meat, you know, in the sixties with the free love and the loose chicks. Excuse me. I mean, you know, those liberated women. But these Japanese nationals, Jesus! I mean, I'm Japanese myself, but these guys, they fucking worship white skin like it's something godlike. Eternal beauty. Fucking unreal. Fucking dumb. Anyways, this guy he likes the tall blonde, he motions her to come in, and she knows the guy is loaded with moola, so she waves in two of her other friends, they're all fucking ugly, I think all women who wear piles of makeup are ugly even if they're really not, I figure they hiding something, you see I like the natural look, hippie-style. So the dumb Japanee tourist is suckered into this thing. He can't back out, he doesn't want to lose favor with the tall blonde, maybe he had her the night before, they seem kind of intimate like they know each other, and so I'm thinking, you dumb Japanee national, you going to have to pay one bill to each of these whores and all you probably will get is to come in one of them. Or maybe they'll blow you off and let you come in the hotel bed sheets, that'll keep their pussies clean for their next fuck. My advice to you is at least get your money's worth. But of course, I don't say anything. That's one no-no. A taxidriver is always a neuter or dumber than his passenger or passengers.

Rule number one. A rule I detest and break all the time. But I don't this time.

Why the fuck am I talking about all of this for? Shit, there's nothing else to do but think like that. Maybe I'll turn the radio on and listen to some of that "New Wave" rock sounds. Christ, what is this shit they have on the radio nowdays? I wonder where's Kammy? God, I'll tell you something. Nothing can take the place of sixties rock . . . yeah! Rah! Rah! Rah!

And here Kammy drives in, parks next to me. Hey Kammy! The buggah is always smiling. Just like the guy on drugs all the time. But I know he don't take drugs. He gets out of his car, yeah, he's going to come in my car and we'll sit and talk, at least have each other's company, this goddamn empty night. Here he comes in.

Let me tell you something about Kammy. The buggah is Chinese. Local, of course, like me. And he's a cabdriver, like me. We both drive the night shift. But the buggah looks like he belongs in another time zone. Just look at him and you'd think you were back in the nineteen fifties. He always wears dark knit pants and the old kind aloha shirts left untucked, and his shoes are always shiny like black glass. Makes you think he's going on one double-date. And look at his hair all pomade-up, slicked back into a ducktail. Hey Kammy! You know, it's the nineteen eighties! Me, I got my hair tied back in a pony-tail. Real radical, no? Well, back in the old days it was. Now, I don't know. People look at me as if I'm a has-been or some-thing forgotten. Back in the old days the long hair blocked a lot of doorways for me, but at the time I thought that was hilar-ious. Funny. Fuck them. And back in those days the long hair opened a lot of other doors. Good friends, beautiful girlfriends who wore no bras and fucked like crazy, nice wine, easy to get into the culture, rock and roll. Christ, was it fun.

Shit. Why am I getting off into this tangent, talking about myself? This story is supposed to be about Kammy. Not me. Why am I talking about myself? Am I insecure or what? Christ.

Well anyway, let me get back to Kammy. His first name is Kenneth, he get one Chinese middle name, then Kam, his fam-ily's name. He told me call him Kammy because that's what all his friends call him. Once he told me the evolution of his name: first it was Kenny, then Kenny Kam, then Ken Kam, then Ken Kammy (sound Scottish, I told him), then just plain Kammy. Since intermediate school. Dole Intermediate. Then he told me about the music group he was in while at Farrington High School. The Two-Tones, they called themselves. Four-part har-mony. "Diana." "Sixteen Candles." "Daddy's Home." The fifties nostalgia. But back then wasn't called nostalgia. Was just plainly called rock and roll. But different from the real rock and roll, yeah? You know, the real rock and roll of the sixties. So I asked him, how come you called your group The Two-Tones when there were four of you in the group? He laughed at me and said, "Actually had six of us." He laughed again. "I tell you why. Us guys, we was all beach boys. Every day after school we make it down to the beach, go surfing. Even cut school, some days. But we was good guys, nevah cause trouble, we use to drink once in awhile, but not the kine drugs like that. Crazy nowdays with all dese drugs all ovah the place, like that. But because we use to surf all the time, we was black like midnight. But under our pants where the sun nevah go under the shorts, we was white-white. Shahk-bait. Our 'ōkoles was white-white. So das why, das why we call our group The Two-Tones."

Kammy. Nice guy. Pākē. Into fifties music. Nice guy. Fellow taxidriver.

So Kammy jumps into my front seat and we shake hands.
    "Kind of slow, eh, tonight?" he says.
    I nod my head. "Yeah, brah."
    "You worked last night?" he says.
    I nod my head. "Yeah. Was slow, but tonight even mo' slow."
    This Kammy, when he's talking sober to me, he tries to speak good English. He knows I went to the University, though I didn't graduate (damn antiwar demonstrations!). And in turn, I try to speak Pidgin, and my Pidgin is rusty cause I nevah speak Pidgin since I waz in grade school, yeah, Kānewai Elementary, and aftah I went grade school my parents wen send me to dat hai-maka-maka private school in town wit' da haoles. Funny, I'm aware of this, but I don't do anything about it. I just let it go. And I think Kammy is aware of this, too, and again, like

me, he just lets it go. Then there are the times when we've drunk a case between ourselves and I go back to my standard English and Kammy goes back to his Pidgin argot, Christ, some real hard stuff, when you listen to him you think you're drinking on the curb in Kam Housing. That's where Kammy's from. Or he used to be from. He told me that he saved some bucks and bought his parents a home in Kalihi.

"I didn't come work last night," Kammy says. "I stayed home. I was thinking." He's staring out my dirty windshield, then looks at me with a seriousness, as if he is going to propose something important or businesslike to me. He does. He says, "You know, Bobby. I was thinking. Maybe you and me we should go into business."

I say, "You talking to the wrong person, Kammy. You know I no like get into the kine business like things. I no like capitalism."

"Yeah-yeah," he says, with an irritated nod of his head. "But you cannot just think like this forever. You gotta think about the future."

"What future?" I say. "The fucking government jus' 'bout going put us in one 'nothah war . . . one nuclear war! Den what? Everything going be dust. Nothing to look forward to."

"There you go in yo' politics again." He laughs a kind of anxious laughter. "Bobby, you gotta be serious about life. Look. Listen to me. No say nothing until I finish."

I nod my head.

"If we can put some cash together, eh, then we can buy couple cars, turn them into taxis and put them on the road. Then we can get some other guys drive them and pay us rent. Easy money. All we do is sit back and collect the rent. And after we get some more money together, we can get more cars and put more taxis on the road. The sky's the limit, brah. Easy money."

Easy money. But where's the seed money? Christ, after paying for the rent of the cab and for gas after every night, I have maybe thirty-five bucks left. And that's on a good night. And part of what's left goes to fast foods and rent for my crummy studio. And of course weed and beer. What do I have left after that? Nothing.

"Nah, Kammy," I say. "Not going work. Not fo' me. Why you no go do 'em yo'self?"

"I could. I would. But you my good friend. I see you in the dumps. I like help you up, get some purpose in yo' life."

I laugh weakly. Kammy is a good friend. Yeah, I'm not in that good of a condition, I have to admit that. But Christ, I'm kind of happy doing what I'm doing now. Well, I'm not that excited about my life, but at least I'm thinking of getting my head together. Maybe when I get my shit together, I'll write that book I've been planning to do for several years now.

"Thanks, brah," I say. "But I cannot do 'em."

"Why?"

"'Cause I think I going start writing my book in little while."

"You been talking about that since I first met you."

That was five years ago.

"I not talking about dreams that not going come true," Kammy says. "I talking 'bout dreams that going come true. I told you about the things I use to do? About the . . . "

Yeah, Kammy. You told me. About owning a condominium, promoting a boxing card, driving around in a Mercedes. When you first told me all of this, I remember looking at you in total disbelief, actually feeling sorry for you. Here I was, with some college education and I know you knew that, listening to you a high-school dropout talking about the big fortune you made in your life. Bragging like crazy. Who's going to believe this guy? I told myself. And if he's so rich, then what is he doing driving a cab? Well, as we continued to see each other in the stands, we began our friendship. And you told me more. I learned that what you had told me was true—or at least most of it was true. So you did own a condominium— well, you once rented a condominium in Makīkī for a couple months; and you were involved in the promotion of a box- ing card—you worked for a boxing promoter once doing advertising work, that is, putting up boxing posters all over the town; and you did drive around in a Mercedes—the box- ing promoter's car. You had chauffeured the promoter to the airport once with instructions to drive it back to the office garage, but instead you detoured and kept the car for a week, driving around town like a self-made man, and when the boss came home prematurely and found out what you had done you were fired. Yeah, there were some major discrepancies to your stories, but the hell with them. At least the fact remained that the stories were close to the truth. And besides, we were both in lonely times and we had a need. And so we got along together, and, though I have never told you because I'm too afraid to say it to your face, you're the best friend I have.

"Kammy, you told me that story already," I say patiently.

"I know," he says. "But you never understand the point what I was trying make."

I let him go. He needs to talk about these things, I think to myself.

Then my mind starts to drift. I start thinking about for- bidden things, like what it would be like if I didn't make cer- tain decisions in my life, where I would be today. If I hadn't flunked out of college. I was smart enough. But I was going to too many demonstrations and smoking too much dope and trying to get into as many panties as possible. Yeah, blame it on the sixties, on the demonstrations and women. I had fun. But the fun is over now. It was over a long time ago. And what if, when I was in school, I majored in something more marketable? Like engineering or computer science. Or architecture. Instead of political science. There was a time I wanted to be a people's lawyer. But that soon faded. The only thing you can do with a political science degree is to go to graduate school. And I didn't even finish my undergraduate years. And anyway, studying about political systems and political theory just got to be boring. Just a rehashing of systems that are always imperfect and never work to their claimed ideals. Jesus, after a while every book started sounding boring.

I sigh. I look over at Kammy. He's still telling me his story, so emphatically, his hands gesturing up storms of controversy in the dead air of my cab, it's like this is the first time he's telling me this story. Or like how an eight-year-old tells his best friend about encountering the biggest fish he has ever seen. Something like that.

But something is missing. It's that look in his eyes. His eyes are sparkling in the dark, once in a while shining brightly with a passing car's light beam. I can see a sadness in his eyes that wasn't there yesterday. He continues telling his story, smiling and laughing in his patented way—his mouth opens, exposing his crooked teeth, his face all scrunching up. Later, much later, with not even a call on the stand phone and the dispatch radio seemingly dead, outside leaning on my cab and smoking our cigarettes, he tells me what is really on his mind. His father died last night. His voice cracks. He tells me that he has not seen his father for over fifteen years, even though his father lives in Kalihi Valley and Kammy lives down the road in

Kapālama. He tells me that his father had disowned him since he came out of the service with a dishonorable discharge, after he had punched out his C.O., which had sent him sixteen months in the brig. I never heard this story about he being in the service and being a rebel and I'm about to say, right on, brah, but I stop short because I see that his eyes are flooding with tears and now they drip-drip-drip down his face, silently. And his face becomes old and softened and wrinkled, and you can tell he's embarrassed that he's crying because he straightens up suddenly and turns away from me, wiping his face and eyes with his hands and sleeve of his shirt. I put my hand on his shoulder, rubbing some comfort, I say, take it easy, brah, everything's going to be all right. And he says, bullshit, brah, my fathah hated me, even when he was dying he nevah wanted see me. And I say, nah, yo' father was jus' 'fraid tell you he like see you, das how fathahs are, and he, nah, brah, he love my bruddah who get his own business mo' den me. And my sistah who married one rich accountant. But me . . . he could care less if I was dead o' alive.

And I'm a bit embarrassed at all of this because I never expected to see Kammy break out of his always jovial mood, I never expected to see a guy like Kammy, a grown man, start crying. I've seen other men cry, no sweat on that. But that was sixties times, man . . . you know, with all that sensitivity to humanism and humanistic psychology and group encounters and therapy and free love and women's lib and all of that. But Kammy? To tell you the truth, I am kind of taken aback to see him cry. He's not supposed to cry. He was raised in an era when men crying is a no-no. Men are not supposed to show their emotions, they are supposed to hide them . . . be men. It's all right for someone like me because I'm from the era that says it's all right. But not for Kammy.

Anyway, I feel sort of bad thinking the way I'm thinking, so I tell him, eh brah, let's take off from work and go up Diamond Head Lookout and drink some beer. And then I remember that I have a couple doobies hidden in a secret fold of my wallet and so I tell him let's go smoke some joints. And he says, clearing his voice and eyes once again, what? yo' weed? you crazy or what? you think I like be one nogood hippie bum like you? And then he starts to laugh. And I laugh, too. Then we get into our cars and before he takes off, he says, I meet you ovah there. And I know he's going to the liquor store and get himself a cold pack of beer because I know he doesn't smoke pakalōlō. So I drive down Kalākaua in the direction of Diamond Head and on the way this young haole chick flags me down and I naturally pull over the side and she gets in my cab and tells me she wants to go to Bobby McGee's and I say to myself, right on 'cause I'm going in that direction, and its a short ride there and I start making small talk to her, I take a couple glances in the back to size her up but this car behind me has his goddamn highlights on and all I can see is her silhouette and I say to myself she's not really talking to me so I guess she's not interested she just wants to get to where she's going and when I drop her off—meter reads $2.40—she gives me two dollars and two quarters, keep the change, shit, ten cents, fuck you, you . . . you . . . you haole. Tourist. Or whatevah.

So I go up to Diamond Head Lookout and get out of my car and I notice several cars in the darkness parked in various conflicting angles to one another, and one particular car has a squeaky suspension and I look at it with suspicion and envy. I go to the wall and sit down, overlooking the cliffs and the waves that I hear roaring below and vaguely see the whitewater by the light of the silvery moon, by the light of the half moon, and I take this thinly rolled smashed joint of Kona Gold

from my wallet and light up. I would wait if I knew Kammy
smoked. And I blow warm nostalgic smoke out for the breeze
to carry to the fucking parked cars, just to let them know what
I got so they can get all green with envy.

Then Kammy drives in and parks next to my car, and he
gets out with a snap, carrying his package, and his car radio
is blasting out the wicked guitar of Carlos Santana—Carlos
baby, I can smell your solos fifty miles away. And I say to
myself:

Carlos Santana? *Abraxas*? Since when Kammy started listening to this kind of music? So he sits down next to me, guz-
zling down a brew, and I expect him to tell me the name of
this particular song, but he doesn't and instead he finishes his
can, crushes it in his hand and tosses it down into the kiawe
brush. Ecology, brah, no make litter, ecology. But I don't say
anything. He's in good spirits and I don't want to rock the boat.
He offers me a beer and I take it, and then he says in his best
haole, nice tune, eh? And then he adds without warning, I
fucked one haole hippie chick one time. I open my beer with
a spurt. Oh yeah? I say. Yeah, brah, he says, was one good fuck.
I try to imagine what kind of girl would fuck him, maybe she
was fat, with zits all over her face. Then I start to get ashamed
of myself for thinking such thoughts. Shit. I feel bad. Oh yeah,
I say again, apologetically, so . . . was good? He nods his head,
smacks his lips, and that episode is over. A short while later
he tells me that he's a father. I nevah know you waz married,
brah? My Pidgin comes out thick, I am forcing it out. Beer:
the drink of the proletariat. Yes, Kammy says. I notice his haole
talk is coming out, though awkwardly. Maybe he used to be
a shoe salesman at Kinney's or somewhere like that, talking
to his customers in the best mainland accent and argot he can
muster. He says, yeah, I'm a father, but no, I wasn't married

to her. He pauses looking out at the ocean. Long moments
pass. I get anxious for him to elaborate more, but I don't press
it. Then he says, I was in high school and used to be in this
church group, one weekend we went to a Christian retreat up
by Mokulēia, I knew her in school, and one night we just went
on the beach to talk story and look at the stars and then the
thing happened, actually she fell asleep and I thought she was
so beautiful the next thing I knew I was on her and doing something I didn't know how to do and then she woke up and
started crying.

We sit there in a windy silence. Then he says, after that night,
I nevah believe in god anymo'. I nod my head and look out
at the ocean, sipping my beer. And then he says, you still get
some of that pakalōlō? And I say shakily and in disbelief, yeah,
and he, well, light it up den!

So I take out my wallet again and take out the last joint and
light up. I give it to him, he asks me for instructions, and I tell
him to take a drag like a cigarette but keep it in your lungs
and count to twenty before exhaling.

He coughs a lot, but soon we are a mile high. I know he's
stoned because we don't talk for an hour. And then he starts
talking.

"Eh, brah, you evah figgah how come some guys get and
some othah guys no mo'?"

And I say with a shrug of my shoulders, "It's because we
live in a prejudiced, unequal society."

"No. Das not the answer I like. I askin' you how come some
get and some no mo'."

And I tell him, "That's what I'm saying. The rich are getting richer and the poor getting poorer because we live in the
richman's system. Capitalism. Sí?"

"Nah, das not what I talkin' 'bout."

And this goes on and on until I finally realize that he's talking from his gut and here I am expounding on my ideas in my standard expository way, and I'm saying to myself do I know what I'm talking about and does he know what he's talking about and then I realize hey! that's all right, everything is all right, we're here discussing and cussing at these matters of political life and whatnot, sitting on this cold rock wall, and the main thing is that we're here and doing this and not not doing this at all. And we continue like this the rest of the night. And I wish that I had another joint to share with my friend.

The phone wakes me up around ten the next evening. I get up, my eyeballs rubberized, and answer the phone. It's my boss, the owner of the cab, and he asks me if I'm coming in or what, and I ask him if it's all right with him if I can take the night off, and he says no. I feel like cursing at him, telling him to go to hell, but I keep quiet and tell him sheepishly that yeah, I'll be coming in. I hang up, drop on the bed, thinking that I had better bounce off the bed before I fall asleep instead of going to work and end up paying the little fucker free money. So I try bouncing off the bed and end up slipping and falling on the floor.

I park at the stand, drinking my large, takeout coffee, my eyes focusing in and out of the darkness. Then the phone rings and I get a fare.

All night I do not see Kammy. He must have had a hangover or something, I think to myself, or maybe he just got too wasted at his first time trying pakalōlō. I laugh to myself. And he always says he never gets drunk.

I do not see him for the next four days. I wonder about him. I start to worry. What happened to him? Then I realize that he probably went to his father's funeral. Yes, I decide, that's where he is. You know Pākē families, they really get into a funeral, it's a big social event with them.

After a couple weeks, I decide to go see him, he hasn't been to work for all this time. The only thing is that I don't know where he's living. All I know he lives somewhere in Kapālama. So I go to the taxi dispatch office and ask for his address.

They have a file on every driver, full with "essential" information. Christ, nowdays everyone has a file on everybody else. It's a police state we live in. I get it reluctantly from one of the dispatchers who owes me something, I turned him on with some of my weed when he was driving cab with us before he became a dispatcher. But the address is a post office box. So I do the next best thing which I should have done first and that is to look in the phone book, and there are several Kenneth Kams and I call them, but they are not the Kenneth Kam I'm looking for, and there are a lot of Kams listed and so I give up, I don't want to call every number in the listing that begins with an 847 or an 845 or an 841, I'm not cut out for that kind of work. So instead I take the bus to Kapālama and check on every apartment building down several, randomly chosen streets, asking for a Kenneth Kam. I do this for one afternoon and then give up. The next afternoon, though, I find where he was living.

It is a small house at the end of a very quiet and narrow lane, rusty wire fences surrounding every house and the smell of fresh dog shit hanging heavily in the air, no wind dares comes into this dismal lane, this I can swear to. I find his house by accident.

Earlier that afternoon, I bump into his brother. He is a shy, soft-spoken guy. I bump into him in the middle of Chinatown. His hands are covered with blood and fishscales. I am at the

open market in Chinatown looking at the fish, trying to
decide what to get for my dinner. It is my night off. I see a
dirty, cob-webbed sign and it says: Kam's Fish Market. My
mind ticks. I see his brother enviserating an aku and I go up
and study this fishgutter, his face has a similarity to Kammy's
though leaner and darker. But still the same snub nose and
thick lips and wide mouth. The fishgutter gets uncomfortable
at me watching him, so I ask him how much for akule and he
says it's a dollar ninety-nine a pound. I ask him if he'd clean
it for me and he says, with a nod of his head, yes. Then I ask
him if he's the owner of this stall and he says no, that his uncle
is the owner that he just works for his uncle, and then I ask
him if he has a brother named Kenneth Kam and he freezes
up, he gives me a strange nervous look as if I'm an FBI agent
or a coyote ready to ask him for his green card. Then he nods
his head fretfully and says, yes, I have a brother named Kenneth,
and his voice is weak and I know he would rather I leave right
this second or not ask him any more questions. So I ask for
two akule and he quickly selects two, shows them to me and
I nod my head, and with a swiftness and efficiency that Hari
Kojima could never match, he cleans them under running
water, wraps them up in pink butcher paper and tells me the
price. I pay him, then tell him I am a good friend of his
brother's and I ask where I can reach him. He tells me that
Kammy used to live in Kapālama and I ask him for the address
and he tells me again he does not live there anymore and he
looks down at the fish he is cleaning and I ask him if he knows
where he moved to and he shrugs his shoulders and I ask him
again if he could give me his address and he then sighs irritably and gives me the address to get rid me.

So I go to the house at the end of this lane. I enter the small
yard, pushing aside carefully an old wooden gate with one

hinge rusted and broken off, and as I climb the narrow wooden stairs to the small porch, I notice three skinny old men staring at me remorsefully with yellowed eyes. I say hi to them but they don't say anything. So I ask them if Kenneth Kam lives here and again they don't say anything. They regard me for a few moments, then go back puffing their cigarettes. The butts they have scattered by the dozens all over the porch's floor, and they stare distantly down the lane at nothing in particular. I knock on the door and after a long wait and couple more knocks this rotund Portuguese woman answers the door and she says, "Yeah? What you want, boy?"

I ask her about Kammy and she looks away for a couple of blinks, taking in a deep breath and crossing her heart, then tells me that he doesn't live here anymore. I ask her if she knows where he is, and she says no, that he's living nowhere now. Confused, I ask for clarification.

"Boy, you no read pepah?" she tells me imperiously. "You look like you get college education. You no read pepah or what?"

I tell her, no, I don't read the newspapers. I ask her, why? She shakes her head. "Then you no listen to the radio?"

I am getting anxious. Why is she asking me all of this for?

She says, "You nevah hear 'bout dat mental who wen jump off the building downtown?"

A frightening chill enters my body suddenly. My mouth drops open.

"You talking 'bout Kammy, eh? The Pākē man? He wen jump off one building last week. The buggah wen go lolo all of a sudden. Really, too bad fo' him. He was doing real good, you know. I dunno what happen to him. All of a sudden he wen go nuts. He was one good man . . . him. No make trouble. The only thing he always talking big kind, how he going do this, how he going do that. And das all he do but talk big but no do nothin'. Talk-talk-talk. Das what his problem was. Talk-talk-talk. He couldn't stop. He always talking what he going be.

"Ho! My ear fall out listening to him day-in, day-out. Das why I no listen to him. When he around, I jus' going the othah way. Yeah, das what wrong with him." She averts her eyes to the old men. "But othah den dat, he was all right. No make trouble. At least he wen go out work, make some little bit money, not only freeload from the state like dese deadheads ovah heah." She issues a taunting look at the three men who do nothing in return but gaze with vacant eyes at the fly-buzzing dirt lane.

I can't think straight, my thoughts are all hammajang, but I say, "When is his funeral?"

"Was today. This morning. You miss it already."

I ask where he was buried, she tells me. I leave, thanking her solemnly. I give my best to the boys now watching me depart.

On the way to the gravesite, I am overcome with guilt. Maybe I shouldn't have offered the pakalōlō to him. Maybe that's what threw him off. But I didn't know he was a mental patient, or an ex-one. I didn't know. Kammy, I tell my conscience, hoping somehow Kammy might be listening in, I didn't know, I swear I didn't know you were like that. And why didn't you tell me you were like that? I would still be friends with you. You are my only good friend, Kammy, the others have all gone to become doctors and lawyers and teachers and and and and I cannot take the city bus because I am crying, tears are making my face a mess, I cannot see clearly, and I must take the back roads because I'm afraid someone will see me crying in this . . . this broad daylight, and I would be embarrassed.

I find his grave. The dirt is fresh and warm. I run my fingers into the dirt and apologize to him. My tears are gone, I have cried them all out, but I continue to cry. I imagine my tears falling and dousing his body buried six feet below. There are no flowers on the grave, so I look around and see some withered flowers in a nearby trash can and I go there and pick the freshest and return and place it on the dirt. Then I promise him that I will return the next day and bring him some beer and more flowers. Then I leave.

I do not return to his grave. I am stricken with an inexorable guilt. It exudes from my inner self at all times and invades my thoughts and is destroying my will to live and eat and sleep and even annulling my fantasies of sex with strange and beautiful women. This all will pass, I tell myself constantly, it is not my fault. But I cannot believe myself. I am a goner.

Then Kammy comes to me in a dream and we are laughing and drinking, and then he takes me to the graveyard and I do not want to enter it, I stop at the entrance with a black wrought iron gate, there's a mist that covers the graveyard, real spooky! yah! but he shoves me in and drags me to a freshly dug grave. He pushes me to the edge. I'm struggling back, but weakly. I look down into the hole and it is masterly cut into the dirt, the corners are neat and perfect ninety-degree angles. I can't see the bottom of the hole, it is dark and endless and I feel a warmth rising from it, I smell the smell of earth that has the bittersweet smell of formaldehyde, and the smell is disturbingly alluring and wonderful and makes my body rock back and forth. Suddenly I feel Kammy's cold hand at my neck, grabbing my collar, and he yanks me back and lets go. I am falling backwards, I turn and land on my face, the smell of wet grass stuffs up my nose. Then he kicks my ass and I go flying, knocking my head into an old gravestone. I turn and he is laughing and he shouts, he roars, "Get dah fuck outta here, you fucking hippie!!" And I get up and start running as fast as I can. At the entrance of the graveyard, I stop, turn around, and I see Kammy waving his hand way over his head, and he is far away but I think I can see him smiling.

I've just finished page thirty-eight. It has taken me an entire week to do this. My grammar is atrocious. My spelling worse. But the story is coming out. It is not the original idea I had panning in my head for the past decade or century or whatever time has passed. But the story is coming out, laboriously, but the fuckah is coming out. The story is about life. And that's all I'll say about it. And I know I will continue and finish this book, this novel. There are no dead-end lanes for me now. I've seen enough of them. There are only streets and more streets connecting with the last one—like picking up a fare and dropping off and right at the spot you dropped off you get another fare to take you somewhere else. Only nobody is telling me where to go, I'm going where I want to go. After I finish with this book, this novel, there'll be others. I know there'll be. I can feel it. And I'll dedicate this first book, this first novel, to Kammy. I'll give him the first copy of the book. If it doesn't get published, I'll xerox a copy of it and give him the original, bound. I'll set it on his grave with a cold pack of his favorite beer, pouring out the contents one after another into the ground. Yes, that's what I'll do. My book to him, the beer, a bunch of fresh flowers. And all of my gratitude.

ISHMAEL REED OR ME

"What's this?" she asked.

Caddie was squatting in front of the bookshelves that I had made from three wooden fish crates I found on Kekaulike Street next to the open markets in Chinatown. The soft white kimono that she wore to bed and on lazy Sunday mornings like today was parted by her thighs, revealing her nakedness to the bookshelves. I envied the books. I focused on the tiny blue bamboo leaves printed all over the kimono like long pointy raindrops. I wished I were one of them, touching a part of her body.

"What's *Mumbo Jumbo* about?" she asked. She took the book from the shelf and, with her lips pursed like a siren throwing kisses, blew the motes of dust from the book's spine.

I set the Sunday sports section to the side. "Hey, come over here."

"Who's Ishmael Reed? You know him?" She opened to the title page of the paperback and found the inscription that Reed had addressed to me. "'Seattle, 1977, For David, Best Wishes, Ishmael Reed.'"

She wasn't coming to me.

"What book?" I asked.

"*Mumbo Jumbo.*"

"That's by Ishmael Reed."

"I know," she said matter-of-factly. She turned to the first chapter. "You know him?"

"Sort of. Yeah, I know him."

Well, sort of. I met him at his reading in a Seattle bookstore. He was actually reading another, newly published book. *Mumbo Jumbo* was an earlier one, I believe his first published novel. I didn't have much money then as an undergraduate at UW—I still don't have much—but I was a small kine fan of his and took my copy of *Mumbo Jumbo* for him to autograph. So actually I lied about knowing him, though I did, technically, meet him.

"Come here."

"No."

"Why? Come here."

"No. I'm going to read this book. The cover's kinda interesting. What's it about?"

"Just read it yourself," I said.

"I will."

She didn't talk to me for the rest of that morning. She lounged in her kimono, reading Ishmael Reed's book, lying on her tummy, then moving to her side, then back to her tummy, and on and on, the flaps of her kimono ever so often opening up new nude parts of her body. I tried cozying up to her, but she refused my advances, often with a low growl that meant, "Stop bothering me!"

So eventually I gave up trying to make love to her. I made a brunch of scrambled eggs, toast, bacon and coffee, and she took a short break to eat, but of course she had the book with her, her clear brown eyes behind those black-framed glasses poring over Ishmael Reed's words as if they were some kind of prophecy. I was getting jealous.

"I wish you would read my stuff like you read his," I said finally.

"He's a good writer," she said.

I know she didn't mean it to get at me, but it did. Caddie's comments are never carelessly acerbic but matter-of-fact. At times, by their very nature, they are more trenchant than the usual cuts.

"Why don't you read my stuff?"

"I do."

She did.

"But this guy," she qualified, I thought, rather vaguely, "he's a good writer. He's good."

I tried to hide my jealousy as I ate the last tidbits of scrambled eggs I had made watery by mixing in too much milk. She looked up. "I mean, you're a good writer, hon, but this guy, well, he just puts it all together."

Puts it all together. Damn. What does *that* mean? That I can't *put it all together*?

"Oh." She regarded the wall clock. "I didn't know it was this late." She marked the book with the empty envelope of the latest phone bill and got up.

"We gotta get dressed."

"What for?"

"Jasmine has a party for her son. His first birthday. I told you that . . . last week. Are you coming?"

"I got one choice?"

"No. You promised me you were coming. Let's get dressed. Come on. We're going to be late."

She went into the bathroom, then the bedroom. She came out of the bedroom dressed in a red blouse and blue jeans.

"How come you're not dressed?" she asked.

I sipped my coffee and gave her a smirk, then went into the bedroom to dress.

We made love when we got back, but minutes after we had cleaned ourselves, she put on her white kimono, clicked on the lamp on her side of the futon, and propped herself up with two pillows to read.

"Don't you have to work tomorrow?" I asked.

"Uh-huh. But I want to finish the book. I'm almost finished. Night, sweetie."

I turned away from the light and went to sleep.

Since my first class on Monday wasn't until 10:30 A.M., Caddie usually left before I rolled off the futon. I was a part-time lecturer at Kapiʻolani Community College, using my master's in English to teach developmental writing and freshman composition. I liked the job except for the paper load. Caddie worked as a clerk at a state agency in town. She had a bachelor's in art history and was considered to be an overly educated secretary. But she liked the job. She never complained about it or the people she worked with, though recently she had muttered at least a couple of times that she was interested in going back to school.

I didn't see her until about six that evening. She was carrying a small bag of groceries. I also noticed Ishmael Reed's book sticking out of her handbag.

"What you got?" I avoided looking at her bag, which she had set down next to the groceries on the kitchen table.

"Milk. Bread. Dinner."

"What you going to make tonight?"

"I bought some fish."

"What kind?"

"Your favorite."

Akule. Pan-fried. With shoyu on top. But I wasn't salivating.

"I thought you finished the book," I said finally.

"I did, but I wanted to find his other books at the bookstore and didn't want to forget his name, so I brought along the book," she explained, as she emptied the bag. She placed the styrofoam tray of akule on the counter, the bread next to the toaster, and the other items in the refrigerator. "The bookstore downtown didn't have any of his books. Where did you get *Mumbo Jumbo*? Oh right, you got it in Seattle."

"At a used bookstore," I said, purposely trying to degrade the book. But she didn't catch on to my symbolic reference.

"You made rice?"

"Yeah."

I sat at the table and watched her spread a section of Sunday's newspaper over the counter, then open the tray of akule. She began cleaning the fish. Well, at least she's cooking something I like. Maybe I'm taking this Ishmael Reed thing to the extreme, I thought. I decided to change my attitude.

"Maybe you can find one of his books at the UH bookstore. Or the public library. I know you can find his books at Hamilton Library."

She turned to me, her expression one of surprise and spark. "Hey, that's a good idea. You think the UH bookstore is still open? How about Varsity Books? You think it's still open?"

"Don't know." I thought that perhaps I shouldn't have given her the idea.

"Do you want to go after dinner?"

She returned to cleaning the fish. I should have been pleased that she was making one of my favorite dinners, but I wasn't. In fact, I was feeling worse. I had actually given her the reason to read more of his books. Why did I get him to autograph my copy? It wasn't that great of a book.

"Yeah, I guess so," I said. "We can go after dinner. But only for a little while. I got some work to do."

"And you got dishes."

"Yeah . . . right."

"I can go by myself."

"No, I'll go. Right after I do the dishes."

"You sure?"

"Yeah, I'm sure. Right after dishes."

"All right. You want a beer?"

She had called the two bookstores and both were closed. So she called the bookstore at Ala Moana Shopping Center. The clerk told her, after checking on the shelf, that there was one copy of what the clerk thought was his best book (which I found out to be the one he read in Seattle). So she drove down to the shopping center, with me tagging along, went to the bookstore, and purchased the copy. The look on her usually passive face was that of a child opening Christmas presents. She was happy.

I couldn't understand it, but somehow watching her happiness made me happy too. Well, sort of. I was surprised I felt that way. I guess I thought I should've been a few degrees more jealous. We went to get something to drink at a nearby coffee shop.

"How was work?" I asked. She was already digging into the new book.

"All right. Janice is going to have a new baby, and Irene's son just got into MIT. He's the smart one at 'Iolani." She was telling me all of this while reading the first chapter of the new Ishmael Reed book.

How can she do this? I thought. I was getting a bit bothered.

"Hey, you want to talk to me, or what?"

"Huh?" She looked up at me. She was beautiful. Sexy.

"Oh," she said. Somehow she caught on to what I was feeling. She sipped her coffee and quietly put the book back into its paper bag. "What were you saying?"

"I was asking you about work."

"I thought I answered you."

"Well, you did. But not really."

"Why? Well, how was your work?"

"Why do you like him so much?"

"Like who?"

"Like him." I pointed to the paper bag.

"I like the way he writes," she said, pretending to be oblivious to my jealousy. "I like his writing. He's a good writer." She paused. "I don't know him, so I don't know if I like him, personally."

"You seem to like him a lot."

"His writing." She smiled, more of a smirk, but a cutie-pie kind. "You're a good writer, David, but he's a good writer, too."

Too? "A better writer?"

"Well, he's published."

"I've been published, too. In *Hawai'i Review* and *Bamboo Ridge*. I got a story in both of them."

"I know, and they're good stories. But . . . you should read his stuff."

"I did read his stuff. Why do you think I have that book you just read?"

"Well, yeah, I know. David . . . why are you getting all irritated for?"

"I'm not irritated."

She smiled at me, that Caddie-like kind of smile: her lips pursed just a bit, the corners of her mouth suggesting compassion and passion at the same time. Why the hell was I getting all futless?

We went back to the apartment. I sat with my pile of papers to correct at the kitchen table while she retired to the bedroom . . . with her new book. By the time I had finished my work, a few minutes past midnight, she was already sleeping. I took a long hot shower. I turned on the TV and watched some late-night shows, hosted by flaky hosts for hosts of flaky people, before turning in. I turned on my lamp and watched Caddie sleeping quietly. Her back was towards me, and I could see the soft rise of her breathing. I slowly uncovered her of the comforter. Her kimono was bunched up, showing her legs and the bottom of her panties. I softly touched the folds of her body. I wanted to wake her and make love to her. But I didn't. I glanced at the book resting at the base of her lamp. A marker was placed halfway into it.

By the time I got up she was gone to work. I hadn't even heard her get up and get ready. I glanced at my clock. I had an hour to get ready for my morning class. I looked over on her side again. The book was gone.

Driving to work, my mind was not at all focused on my class. I was determined to confront her with this predicament. But was I taking this to the extreme? Why was I feeling this way, and just over a stupid book, over a writer she'd probably never meet? Why was I so threatened by Ishmael Reed?

Hey! I'm a better writer than he! I'm a better lover! He can't make Caddie come so many times like I can! I can make her come two, sometimes three times a try. No ways he could ever do that with any woman! Hey! Caddie is mine! Mine! Mine!

I couldn't find a parking stall. I circled the lot about three times, the unobtrusive morning sun beginning to turn into a sweltering one, and finally decided to sit and wait for an opening. Damn. Damn Ishmael Reed. He's the damn reason why I can't find a parking stall. And for my being late for class. Goddamn Ishmael Reed and your books.

I started thinking about what Caddie was doing at the moment. She was probably taking her coffee break with you know who. I was getting madder and madder, my mind getting more and more heated up under the hot sun. Was this driving me crazy? Yes. Yes, it was.

Tonight. It had to be tonight. I'd lay it on her. *Stop reading Ishmael Reed's stuff and read mine!* Yes, that's what I'd do.

My first session wasn't going well. Almost half the class didn't turn in their assignments. I was pissed.

"Okay, everyone. Take out a piece of paper for a pop quiz," I barked out.

There was a slew of sighs and regrets and under-the-breath swearing. I didn't care. I was on a mission. Don't you tread on me. I'm the teacher, you're the student. If you're not prepared, then so be it . . . you suffer.

I got home in the early afternoon pretty tired. I went to the bedroom, stripped to my boxers and collapsed on the futon, falling to a deep sleep almost instantly.

I woke up in semi-darkness with the Miles Davis Quintet playing softly on the turntable in the living room and something tickling my cheek. It was Caddie. She was lying by my side, watching me and tickling my cheek with the ends of her long black hair.

"You're an angel . . . when you sleep," she said.

I grunted, then closed my eyes. "When did you get home?"

"Just a little while ago. You're such an angel."

"You mean I'm not an angel when I'm not sleeping."

"No. You're an angel when you're sleeping. I like watching you when you sleep."

I was going to tell her the same but decided not to. Didn't want to change the quiet mood we were in. It was nice.

"Let's go out to eat," she said.

"All right." I was still feeling groggy. I needed that sleep. All those nights of not getting my eight hours had added up. "Where you want to go?" I asked.

"I don't know. Anywhere."

"Oh. I thought you'd want to stay in and read."

She giggled.

"You're jealous," she said.

"Jealous? Jealous of what?"

"You know. My reading Ishmael Reed." She gave me one of those Caddie kind of smiles.

"Why should I be jealous?"

"Just to let you know, I stopped reading that second book. Wasn't as good as his first. In fact, kinda bored me."

"Huh?"

"I read about halfway through, but wasn't as good as his first one. So I just stopped reading."

"Oh." I closed my eyes again. "So you wasted your money. . . . "

Her hand slipped down to my groin and began gently rubbing my sweet spot. I held my breath for a moment, absorbing the tingle in my body, then relaxed. "So . . . you wanna go . . . out and eat?"

She didn't answer me. She kissed me. Darkness unfolded on us.

We ended up eating in, opening a couple of cans of chicken noodle soup. But it was the tastiest canned soup I ever ate.

A MEMORY FOR MARTIN

The funeral service for Martin Rapoza, a community badboy—drug addict, liar, thief, father of seven illegitimate children from Kānewai, Hawai'i, to Portland, Oregon—wasn't supposed to be long. What made the funeral long was the surprisingly interminable line of people that had formed during and after the service, wishing to see (or curse) Martin for the last time and console his grieving family—his mother and father, and five sisters and three brothers—who were all dressed in white. The line ran down the center aisle of the clapboard church and out the front entrance; down the wide, groaning wooden steps; and out into the unusually cool summer evening, zigzagging its way diagonally across the large rectangular yard to one corner where the children's playground—erected one drizzly winter Saturday morning by members of the church and consisting of a jungle gym and three swings—was situated. (At the corner of the yard nearest to the church's entrance was the well-maintained community cemetery.) Children were flying all over the yard in this dawning of evening, playing chase-master or tag, or exaggerating the moves of one of their fathers' favorite professional football player. And prodding their young daughters on the swing set, two teenage pregnant mothers were cooing pleasurably in meaningless small talk. Most of the people in line were dressed in their Sunday best, and some were in their everyday dungaree work clothes, sans grease and dirt. Everyone's hair was nicely combed, mostly fixed with pīkake-scented pomade, or pressed together with pins and hairspray. It was a mixed bag of body smells and perfumed airs that exuded from this crowd. And it was nothing short of noisy, this crowd of people who made its way to this modest church, reconstructed in 1929, to this funeral for one of the most notorious of the community's bad boys. (Built in 1876 by a Catholic priest from Portugal who impregnated a thirteen-year-old Hawaiian girl and became a father at fifty-four of a son, the original building was burned down because of a feud between Jared DeCosta and Samuel Souza, who was the grandson and only descendant of Henrique de la Souza, that aforementioned Portuguese Catholic priest. Samuel was crushed to death in the nave by a fiery collapsing roof.)

A sampling of comments was heard from the crowd:

"And den he threw 'em in dah gutter, dah next ball, but dah ball when flip off dah side, jump in dah lane, and den right 'cross and clip dah left split and dah left split when slide ovah and hit dah other split! Nebah see not'ing li' dat befo'! Dah buggah, I owe him fifty dollah, dah sonavabitch!" So said Dexter Napatel to his neighbor Sonny Pico. The line ahead of them mumbled and moved forward. Sonny gave Dexter a nudging look, and Dexter took the first step up the stairs.

At the swings, Shantelle Lee soothed the rolling movement in her belly with one hand while the other carefully pushed her daughter Rachelle. "So how long you and Ray been married?" she asked Terri-Ann Naʻehuiwa.

"One year," Terri-Ann offered, then added after a catch and push, "and eleven months."

Shantelle smiled at Terri-Ann's two-year-old daughter, Brandy, then gave her own daughter a push.

Seven-year old Jeremy Thom tripped up a five-year old Justin Rapoza and gave him a taunting laugh.

"I going tell Uncle Marty on you!" Justin whimpered.

"Nah! You cannot!" Jeremy razzed. "Uncle Marty is dead!"

"Not!"

"Yes-yes! Why you t'ink yo' Mommy is crying fo'? Stoo-pid!"

"I not stoo-pid!"

"Crybaby!"

"I not!"

And Cheetah, who wasn't at the funeral but at home, watching a videotaped Monday night football game that he had viewed twice before, was brooding heavily and addressing himself from time to time on how he was going to get back the seven-hundred-fifty dollars that he had fronted to Martin a couple of weeks before, money which Martin supposedly used to finalize a drug deal that would have brought back Cheetah at least three times the borrowed amount, or so he was told. Cheetah, slouching on a beery-smelling old couch, lit a cigarette, then let out a ponderous but half-affected cheer when his team got an eight-yard gain on a fullback run, a weak attempt by him to forget his guilt for not attending the funeral. (Though Cheetah's alibi was that his car had blown a head gasket, he wouldn't have gone anyway even if he could.)

By the time the last of the family and friends had passed by the open casket (where the mortician's pallid makeup was not laid on thick enough to cover the deep radiated bruises on Martin's face), condoling and hugging the weeping but tear-less family members, it was deep night, and the party that was to follow on the next day was postponed to one week later, to the following Saturday.

The night before the party it rained with spiking thunder, and the weather reporter on Activision NewsTeam Three forecast continuing thunder showers through the weekend. The diminishing trades would situate the rain clouds prettily on the island chain. But somehow in the early morning Saturday, the precipitation dissipated and the sun rose promis-ingly hot over Kānewai. Martin's father and two of Martin's three brothers (Abe, the oldest, was sleeping with the rusty air conditioner on full blast; he had come home to his studio apartment from his early morning gig as a bouncer at a down-town strip joint that showcased Vietnamese, Filipino and haole women) set up the wide blue tarp against the threat of rain or sun, while Ma and Auntie Hennie and daughters and nieces and cousin Aram were inside getting the food ready. And all were anxiously awaiting the removal of the two-hundred-pound-plus pig from the backyard imu.

A heavy but brief shower came from the mountains. More family arrived. Then, about a few minutes past ten o'clock, a late model two-door Subaru sedan drove up the long grav-elly driveway to the house, the narrow driveway lined on both sides with springy green ti leaves that slapped and splashed the car all over with the warm remnants of the rain. At the top of the driveway the road opened up into a wide farm lot, with the Rapoza house—a one-story, white tract farmhouse built in the late 1940s—sitting on one far end next to a rock-hard, ancient mango tree and a hollow, languidly spreading li chee.

The Rapoza homestead was higher than the other farm lots, and on hot sunny days from the porch of the house the entire valley looked crisp and green and relaxing, the scene punctuated with occasional barks and rooster crows, and perhaps distant grunts and squeals from the slaughterhouse near the creek.

The car was driven by Fielding Lee, the forty-five-year-old bachelor math teacher at Wilson High, who had been asked to bring along his flute for a jam session. Of course, he didn't go by the name of Fielding, but by his nickname, Sang. When he was in elementary school, the only child of a single parent, Annie Lee, the school kids teasingly called him "Feeling Lee" or "Feel Lee," both of which he disliked. So he asked his mom to give him another name, and Annie, adamant that his first name not be changed as it represented the only organic attachment she had with her part-Hawaiian lover who had perished in a Solomon Island jungle fighting for the cause of American Imperial Justice, told her teary son that he could be called Sung Juk after her brother, who had also died fighting in the same war, attacking a German unit halfway around the world in France. Sang was at first called "He Sung Junk," but after several playground fights, all of which he lost, he gained his classmates' respect because of his tenacious, never-say-lose pugnacity, something that later he would attribute to Uncle Sung Juk, whom he had never met but would discourse with via a sepia photograph of him in his army uniform. (The photo was framed in koa and set in a respected spot, left-center of the piano top; at right-center was a full-length picture of Charles Kekoaʻaliʻinui Fielding, also framed in koa, strumming his ʻukulele next to the boot camp gate, Georgia.) Eventually his classmates called him "Sang," with no teasing intended, and that was that.

Martin was no friend of Sang, but Sang was close to Martin's older sister. They had been friends while at Wilson High, and both remained the best of friends to the present despite thorough pestering by both the Lee and Rapoza families for them to marry. (Why they never did no one knew, not even Sang or Melody Rapoza.)

Sang parked his car under the mango tree weighed by a bumper crop of green fruit but felt uneasy upon realizing that the oil-soaked spot had been Martin's; there was a strange tingling he felt, as if the idling of the ghost car was right on his lap. So he reversed and reparked his car next to Melody's cream-colored Toyota. It was very unusual that Martin's aqua-blue '65 Mustang was missing—it was like church service without the offering plate—but of course he did remember that the car had been totalled in the freak accident. Martin, in some crystal-meth rage, had tore down the winding narrow road along the Waipuna coast that terminal night, and he continued on, past where the paved road became a dirt one, and proceeded for another mile or two, finally racing his car head-on into an outcropping of black rock. But the crash wasn't what killed Martin. Apparently, Martin had crawled out of the accordion-like wreck—there was not a drop of blood found in the wreckage—and climbed to the top of the rocks, where he dived head first into the lashing waves of the ocean. The next afternoon, when paramedics recovered his body, snagged by the collar of his t-shirt on a bony finger of coral, they found that his neck had been broken. He was also wearing, according to the off-record remark by fireman Wyman Nakakura, the haunting smile of a child who has opened a present the day before Christmas.

Pulling the lever under the dashboard, Sang popped open the trunk of the car. The Dogs Rapoza—Whitey, Brownie,

Beastie and Snory—gathered from the corners of the wide yard and yapped at the arrival of the familiar guest. As Sang got out of the car, seconds after he noticed the flapping salutation of an unattached corner of the large blue tarp and the sweet smoky aroma of kalua pig, a large drowsy fly pecked him right on the forehead. The fly buzzed off and sat on the car's windshield, rubbing its front legs as if taunting him, and before Sang could knock it off it buzzed away, meandering in a lazy roundabout flight over the yard, between and above the leaping snaps of the dogs.

Coming out to the porch, Ma Rapoza waved at Sang, her look long, dry, unforgiving, though her eyes were glinting with a sip of color and promise. She was dressed in a loose taupe shift, and her similarly taupe-colored hair was tentatively held up in a bun by whatever loose energy that was left over from the funeral. Sang waved back, then lifted open the trunk, the hinge squealing with dismal pleasure, and took out the flute and the guava cheese cake that his mother had baked. Balancing the cake pan and instrument case in one hand, Sang used his other hand to close the trunk, bending his legs as the latch snapped. He pleaded with the dogs not to jump on him, which they did anyway, though Brownie's humping action gave him a small thrill. At least they appreciate me, he told himself while scratching their heads with his free hand, at least they like me for what I am.

There was no one in the kitchen, though he noticed signs of unfinished activity: the lid of the rice cooker was rocking on a circle of foamy steam; the warmth of the room was heavy with the aroma of baked ham; the sink was filled with dirty dishes and pots; and the remains of a half-eaten meal were left on the table. He glanced at the dust-draped wall clock, then checked the accuracy of its time with his wristwatch, wondering if he was too early. The kalua pig in the air told him otherwise. He wondered then if he made the right decision to come, remembering the last time he came, during the Christmas holidays, when the youngest brother, Malcolm, was visiting from the mainland with his wife and three children and how an argument had broken out between Malcolm and Martin on why the clocks in the house were all running thirteen minutes behind actual time and why they should or should not be corrected.

No. He wanted to come. To see Melody. Perhaps in this hour of sadness he would tell her the future of his heart. But where was Melody? And where was Ma Rapoza whom he had seen only moments before? (Had he imagined her?) And where was everybody? They must be all in the back with the imu, he told himself. He pictured them all helping out to reclaim the pig from the fire-hardened earth pit the family had used for the high school graduation party for each of the Rapoza children. Yes: To dig out with long metal tongs the steaming lava rocks from the collapsed bowels of the carcass; to peel the translucent oily chips of skin from fat-dripping chicken wire; to crunch on these chips in wondrously warm, oily satisfaction. He didn't feel lonely anymore. They're all waiting for me at the imu, he promised himself.

"Sang?" she called from the living room.

He enters the bare living room with its fresh resinous scent. A gray light from an overcast sky. And there she is, standing in the middle of the room, in a sheer off-white, flowing grown that clings to her full, quivering breasts, nipples erect. Her eyes are dark; her face relaxed and calling; and her long hair, the smacking of midnight, flowing behind her. She reaches across the room and takes him by the hand, pulling him deep into the bosom of the house, down the darkened hallway and into a night of cold blue fire.

Pushing aside plates of food to make room for his offering, Sang set the cake on the table, then went into the living room, feeling the coolness of the smooth dark floorboards through his socks, but at the sight of Melody he stopped. In the middle of the room. She was sitting on the rattan couch on the far wall. She had closed a photo album on her lap, her long slender legs covered partly by a beige-colored, sleeveless dress. She set the album on the coffee table and smiled.

"Sang, how are you? Come over and sit. I haven't seen or heard from you in such a long time. You didn't come to Martin's funeral, did you?"

"No. I . . . was busy that night." He ambled towards her.

"I know. I saw your mother. She looks good. Is she coming to the party?"

He shook his head. "She's not feeling well. Something she ate last night. Something disagreeable with her system."

Melody stood up. Sang noticed the lines around her eyes, a touch of white in her hair, the fullness of face and arms.

"So . . . how have you been?" he asked. He surveyed the room, then looked out the screen door, which led to the backyard. There, the rest of the family was talking and laughing, as if life was all about lifting a pig out of its imu. He smiled at the thought.

"Oh . . . just fine. And you?"

He shrugged his shoulders. "Could be better."

"Sit down, Sang."

He settled on a chair directly across from Melody. Melody sat back on the couch, pushing the photo album to the corner of the coffee table, towards Sang.

"How's your mom taking it?" he asked.

"Oh, she's okay. Between you and me, I think she had been expecting this for a long time already. It was no shock for her. Just wondering when it was going to happen was what really got to her."

Sang nodded knowingly. They all knew Martin was going down the path of tragic death. It had been written in the stars. It was told in the way the cards had fallen for Ma. A month after Martin was born, she had gone to see that old Portuguese woman who lived on the slopes of Punchbowl. In 1891, as a girl of seven, Martha Reveirios had had a vision of thick snow falling and smothering a land covered with a fresh flow of lava, and then another vision of monster 'ahi surrounding and swallowing an entire school of red fish, visions that were told to a lady-in-waiting who had retold them to the Queen. The fortuneteller did not tell Ma Rapoza about the way the baby, who at the moment was sucking hard on a soggy breast, would perish; in fact, this was the second time she refused to tell anyone exactly what she saw. (The other time she had held back telling about the dream of the Queen's face melting to her own feet.) But Ma Rapoza read the sign in the soothsayer's hesitation between the last shuffles, and those seconds of betrayal forged the nightmares that Ma Rapoza was to have for the rest of Martin's life, despite the air of opportunism she always showered on everyone, especially on Martin, about Martin's formidable accomplishments and his promising, star-lit future.

"But let's talk about other things," Melody said. She leaned back, crossing her arms over her chest, her arms lowering then rising with her breathing. For a moment, a tenseness crossed her face, then she relaxed, as if a cramp had come and gone.

"Are you okay?" Sang asked.

"Yes." She smoothened a wrinkle on her lap. "Let's talk."

Sang nodded his head, but before he could say anything, she said, "Why did you come here, Sang?"

Sang's eyes engaged with the pattern of peonies in the throw rug under the table. A burst of laughter outside was now very far away, making him feel isolated.

"I don't know," he said, looking up into Melody's moistening eyes. "I thought that you'd want me to come. Maria called me up the other night. She told me to come. I thought you wanted me here."

"Maria . . . " Melody rolled her head slowly and stared disconsolately out the door.

Another burst of laughter.

"If you don't want me here, I'll go." He moved up to the edge of the chair.

"No . . . stay. Ma wants you here. You know you're always welcome."

"I don't feel it."

"Stay."

She reached over the coffee table and touched Sang's hesitant hand. Sang's eyes drifted and then linked with Melody's. Their minds excluded everything outside their vision. Outside the pig's smoking carcass was being broken apart, its warm buttery flesh falling off bone and being dumped into dimpled aluminum tubs.

That she had carried for the life of her the exacting prophecy of this ending was no one's understanding but Ma Rapoza herself and her three daughters, Melody, Missy and Maria (pronounced Mah-rye-ah). Or so Ma thought.

Outside another car arrives, greeted by the barking of the dogs. A car door slams shut. Seconds later the trunk slams shut.

"Eh Whitey! Eh Brownie! Eh! Get off my clean clothes! Beat it!" The front screen door bangs against the stop. "Anybody home? Auntie Sookie? Uncle Herman?" The guest enters the living room. A smile connects dimples on a broad sun-reddened face. "Eh howzit, cuz!" The guest strolls across the room, embraces and exchanges kissing cheeks with Melody. Melody turns to Sang: "Sang, this is my cousin, Ronnie."

Ronnie extends a short thick arm towards Sang. They shake hands. Sang notes Ronnie's calloused palm.

"Eh I met you befo', yeah?" Ronnie says. "Dah New Year's Party dis past Christmas?"

"I think you mean the Christmas party."

"Yeah-yeah, mus' be. Dah Christmas Party. When Mally wen get kinda lōlō. Heh-heh. You one school teachah, right?"

"Yes."

"I remembah you. Eh good to see you." Turning to Melody: "So wheah everybody? Us'side? Ho, I smell dat peeg! Smell like dey jus' wen take 'em outta da imu. Ho, hungry already! I smell 'em when I was coming up dah road! Dah smell all around dah valley!"

"Yes, they're all outside. Why don't you go outside and help yourself, Ronnie."

"Don't mind if I do. I see you folks later."

He goes to the screen door, takes a deep breath of the smoky aroma, then stops and turns. "Eh almost forgot my slippahs dah other side."

Melody offers a weak smile.

"Guess I'll go out from dah front way. But befo', gotta use yo' lua." Smiles.

Melody returns the smile.

He finds the bathroom down the hall and softly closes the door behind. A faint scent of potpourri. A window open to a fresh breeze. The smell of the piggery. The smell of the loamy earth and California buffalo grass. The smell of kalua pig. Dat Martin. Da fuckah still owe me money. Zips open and yanks out his penis. Scratches his gonads. A strong steady release. Strong smell. Too much drink last night. Where I went last night? Oh yeah, Chalky's. Ugly chicks. How I going get my money back? A picture of "JEsus is WATCHing over YOU toNIGHT" on the bare white wall above the tank of the toilet. Looking up to the side with puncture marks in his open, upturned palms. A spare roll of toilet tissue in a maroon and tan crocheted cover. Please Jesus, and Mother Mary too, help me get my money back. "Amen." Shakes, zips up and flushes. Rinses his hands and wipes them on the back of his jeans. Rusty olive-black door knob refuses to release. Forces it open and enters the hallway. Stops and sneaks a look down towards Martin's room. Laughter outside. Glances towards the living room. Nobody going know. Pads halfway down the hall. Auntie Sookie laughing outside. Nah. Bettah not. Turns. Turns back again. Nah. Auntie's house. Goes back to the living room. "Eh, see you us'side, cuz." Loser cousin, staying wit' dat glass-balls. Should have got married already, long time ago, have kids. Dah fucking guy no mo' dah balls to even ask her get married. Losers, both of dem. And dey think dey so hot, bettah dan me cause dey school teachers. Fuck, I stroke mo' wahines in one week dan he evah had hes lifetime.

Seven strides and he's in the kitchen. Five more and he's out the front door. A mess of slippers and muddied, worn shoes. Smears of mud all over the scuffed wooden porch steps. Squeezes his toes into the tight straps of a pair of newly acquired rubber zoris. The ones he took from his sister's house. Who knows to whom they belonged. They were new, a bright blue with green streaks. His toes could smell—feel—the new when they first wiggled into them. His old pair so thin he could feel sharp gravel poke into his soles. Never mind that they were a couple of sizes too small. His feet would stretch them out, no doubt about that. Or so he thought. Three months later, the soles worn thin, the straps were still pulling at the coarse hairs of his toes. Time fo' one nada new pair.

Boy, dah pig smell good. Pats the rolls of fat over his stomach. Thirsty too. Where Auntie hide dah beer? Looks for the cooler. Where dah cooler stay? No such thing. Brownie and her new pups come out from under the house, her eyes sleepy, cautiously friendly. Squats and plays with the pups. One . . . five. One pure black. Another one white. Two brown with white spots. One runt, one brown one. Turns the runt over and scratches the soft vulnerable pink belly. Fleas scatter to the four corners of the belly. Brownie tries to lick him on the face. "No, Brownie. Get away." The pups paw him on the arms, trying to jump on him, their thin claws needle-sharp. "You runt. You bettah drink yo' mommy's milk and get big, or else yo' brothahs and sistahs going give you lickings all yo' life. Jus' like me. Hootch!" Rises and follows the sweet smoky smell of the pig. Scans the banana patches below, and the piggery and farm lots. A column of smoke rising lazily two or three lots away. Then another, in the distance. A cock crows. Pigs grunting. A squeal. More squeals. Dogs barking. A cow bellows close by.

Sky so nice. Jus' like one painting, dah sky. Fo'evah and evah, Amen. Jus' like one painting.

Turns the corner of the house and sees the clan. His heart lifts. The family. The smells of good food. Approaches the imu with a grin. Auntie sees him, beckons him over: "Ronnie. Come. We need yo' help. Where yo' mothah? She came?"

"Hi, Auntie."

A hug and kiss. Greets the rest of the family.

"No, she nevah come. Maybe later, she said. She jus' recovering from her cold."

She motions: "Come. Pick. Eat."

"Yeah-yeah."

"Yo' sister coming?"

"Yeah, she said she coming. Later."

"Come. Eat."

They were silent while Ronnie passed them. Melody's eyes had followed Ronnie across the living room, through the walls of the house (the trail of noises he made outside: grumbling about something at the porch, talking to the dogs) and then her eyes looked through the screen door to the smoldering imu and caught him greeting the family.

Sang saw anger in the hardening of Melody's dark brown eyes. Her hands began to tremble, and her breath shortened.

"Are you all right?" he blurted out. "Are you feeling ill?"

"Yes. No . . . I mean, yes. Just . . . angry."

"Angry at what? Why are you angry?"

"Angry at—at—that *thing!*"

Her eyes were pressed on the object that was now kissing her mother.

Sang watched her watching him. "What thing are you talking about?"

She turned, glaring at him: "*You* know." She returned to the scene outside. Sang noticed a twitch in her jaw, a quiver on her lips. "I didn't think he had the guts to come here. And I know what he wants." She shook her head, then breathed over the coffee table, her eyes unfocused and wet. "He killed my brother. You know that, don't you?" Her eyes rose to his, begging for a confirmation.

Sang decided not to give it to her.

"You know that, don't you? That *he* killed my brother? And he comes here and thinks nothing of it, as if he were scott-free from any blame. How can a man live with such a burdensome guilt and act that way?"

The photo album provided a focus for Sang's tentative eyes. The cover was pebbled, like the skin of a football. Was this an album of Martin's Greatest Hits?

He had a lot of promise, that Martin. Carried his football team to the divisional championship game, which they won, blowing away their opponent. He had scored four touchdowns in the game.

Sang turned to face the kitchen and was able to see part of a picture frame mounted on one of the walls. The glass of the frame reflected the image of the kitchen window; he knew that the picture frame encased the all-star selection article from the daily newspaper. Martin had been voted Offensive Player of the Year of the league. He was offered a scholarship to a small liberal arts college in Oregon, accepted it, but came home after a year, failing miserably in his school work. Then it was a hitch to Vietnam. And downhill ever since.

Sang remembered one late night when he and Melody were strolling down Waikīkī after a movie. He happened to see Martin, home on leave, and Ronnie cruising down Kalākaua Boulevard in Ronnie's sky-blue VW bug and trading tokes at the red light. They were laughing and choking in the car's smoky interior, not caring one bit that they might be pulled over by one of the many cops patrolling that edgy Waikīkī night. Sang quickly directed Melody's attention to the closest display window.

"Beautiful, isn't it?"

"What, Sang? What are you talking about? Which one is beautiful?"

Melody's mind is dazzled by glittering diamonds and vibrant rubies, the warm shine of various gold rings. Celery-colored jade. Her eyes have wakened from the midnight blues of a just-so movie. Her heart leaps from the bottom of her stomach to the very top of her soul, making her dizzy with a raw delight that she knows comes once in a lifetime, an experience that she has visualized many, many times, one that she has obediently and patiently waited for—too patiently, too many times, perhaps—an unforgettable moment that she senses might just be happening right now.

Oh, Sang! Which one? Tell me! *You* need to tell me, right now!

Sang glances in the feared direction. The traffic light changes, and the cars move on. He can smell the burning weed. They might circle Waikīkī and come back again, he thinks.

"Let's go, Melody. It's getting late."

"Wait. What's the hurry?"

"We better get to the car before it's too late."

"Too late for what? You don't have to feed the meter. It's too late, silly."

"Let's go. Quick. It's getting late."

"Sang . . . "

"Come on, Melody. Let's go."

"But . . . why? Let's look. I don't care which one, Sang. Any one will do."

"Huh? Come on. Let's go."

It's a slow, very slow drop into an insensate darkness, and at times the walls of the descending tunnel flash with images of cupboards and curtained windows that *should* be, and sometimes the cupboards are open and bare, and sometimes they are filled with wonderfully sparkling crystals, unimaginably brilliant and wondrous, sapphiric white and yellow and blue. But it's a slow drop, almost imperceptibly slow, though the stomach might feel it the most, as the dropping exasperates the gloom that holds the tongue, unevens the eyes, and butchers the desire that has become so burdensome.

And she waits so desperately for the crash, for the bottom of this fall, this finality, which she hopes will crush her existence. But the bottom does not come. And, too, the fall is too soft and slow, like a feather drifting down through windless air, a deliverance that brings no physical pain but a narcotic-like stupor.

And she waits. She waits. She waits.

What happened to him? He had everything going for him. College football scholarship. He had this future chiselled in stone. Was it really Ronnie? Vietnam? The New Year's party when a blast of firecrackers sent him cowering under the table of food. He broke one of the table's legs, and all the food on the table got mixed together like chop suey. What a scene. Something was wrong with him. Something was giving. Something had changed. He wasn't Martin anymore: the crewcut, church-going, scholar-athlete whom everyone seemed to admire. He had everything going for him. You just couldn't get jealous of him, he wouldn't allow it with his always smiles and his just being the good guy he was. Something happened to him overnight. Vietnam? During his first year in college? Perhaps a head injury in a football game? What? And now—or was—an ice addict and dealer.

"I hate him."

Sang studied Melody's profile, the frigidity of her lips pursed by the words. Her hair, with weak streaks of gray, flaring back like shards of angry flame. She could be Pele, Sang thought, the fire goddess attacking her sister Hi'iaka for supposedly stealing her lover.

"Why are you looking at me like that? You make me feel like a child. I . . . I don't like it."

Melody lowered her eyes. Sang looked towards the imu. Ronnie, chomping on a chunk of pig flesh, dripping with fat, was listening to Ma Rapoza.

"It wasn't his fault," Sang said calmly. And immediately he regretted saying what he did.

"What do you mean? That jerk killed my brother. He got him addicted to all those drugs. I know. How could you be— be a good person, someone the whole community loved and respected, then overnight turn into a—a—a monster?"

"He's not a monster." Sang realized his use of the present tense. He continued: "He's your brother."

"I know he's my brother. But so what. He became a monster. He stole from Mama. He stole from me. He lied to me, on and on. He's my kid brother, and he lied to me. I loved him. And it's all because of that—that *shit* out there."

As if in an attempt to kill him, she stared hard at Ronnie, who had just finished sucking his fingers and was now helping himself to more pig flesh. Sang noticed for the first time the auburn tinted ends of Melody's hair. She was taking a different look. A small fright entered Sang, then left, leaving traces of a chill.

"How can you defend that creep? You know how my brother was. Right?"

Sang nodded his head, was about to say something but stopped himself, wondering why that thought had come to him. He reconsidered the worth of his reticence and said, "But how can you deny what was once real, that has now turned into a dream?"

The phone rings.

She hears the tinkling through the rush of steamy water that rinses the rich lather from her body, that lifts and runs off the dirt and stress of the working day. She turns down the shower and listens for the ring, hesitates, daring herself to run dripping and naked to the phone. No, she will not. She will let it ring. If it is important, the party will call again.

She turns up the water and falls back into this steamy pleasure, re-rinsing her long black hair that touches her buttocks. She runs her hands over arms, breasts, stomach, legs, rubbing off the soapiness from the skin until it resists touch. Her fingers gently and firmly cleanse her vulva and anus with falling water.

She shuts off the water, twirls her hair into a rope to squeeze the excess water, then pushes aside the shower curtain and steps out, taking a fresh towel and burying her face into its scentless fluffiness. She has only rubbed out the drippings from her hair when the phone rings again, this time with a seemingly hard urgency. She wraps her body with the towel and tosses her hair behind, tiptoes quickly to the phone and answers it.

"Martin coming home." It's her mother.

She catches a small breath. "Oh. That's good."

"He leaving school."

"What do you mean?"

"He quitting school."

"Why?"

"He said school not fo' him. I dunno . . . I think something must've wen happen. But he no tell me nothin'."

"What happened to him?"

"I dunno. He nevah say nothin' to me."

"Did he get hurt? Did he get injured playing football?"

"I have no idea."

"Did he flunk out?"

"I dunno. His first semester he did okay. He had all B's and C's."

"A 2.3 GPA."

"Something like that. You talk to him when he come home. Maybe you can change his mind."

"Yes, I will. I'll talk to him."

Silence.

"Ma, what's the matter? Ma, don't worry. I'll talk to him."

"Is not him leaving school that bothering me. Is the way he told me about it."

"What do you mean?"

"He said the man at the waterfall told him he cannot come back. I ask him, 'What you mean?' But he nevah answer me. You know what he means by that?"

"I don't know. You sure you heard him right? Ma, don't worry. I'll talk to him. Ma, can I call you later? I just got out of the shower and I'm dripping wet. I'm dripping all over my living room."

"You call me back? Right away?"

"Yes, Ma. I call you back right after I dry myself and dress."

"Okay. You call me back. You okay?"

"Yes, Ma. I just got home. Had a tough day at school, so I just wanted to take an early shower. Don't worry. I'll call you right back."

"Okay."

"Bye, Ma."

She hangs up the receiver, stares at the phone for a moment, then sits on a favorite chair, the one she found one Saturday morning at a garage sale in Kāhala and reupholstered herself in an Alan Akana-designed red anthurium print fabric. She brings her knees to her chest. A breeze has slipped into the apartment, chilling her. For a long while she remains in this position, looking out the window from her seventh-floor condo at dull white clouds. The towel loosens. She feels herself becoming smaller, and smaller. And when her damp hair has softened and the towel has fallen completely from her body, she whispers, "Why?"

"What is it, Booboo?" Melody asks, sleep in her voice. It is two days before Christmas and not a time to be sad, but Martin has come to her bed rubbing eyes that are drippy with tears. He sits at the edge of her bed. She yawns. It is still dark outside. It must be about five o'clock in the morning.

"What's the matter, Booboo?"

Martin continues to sob.

"Daddy wen spank you?"

Martin shakes his head. Melody thought she heard Daddy getting up to go to work. And Mama too. Mally is still sleeping. She can hear him buzzing in the next room.

"Booboo, what's the matter? You had a bad dream?"

Martin nods his head, wipes the tears from his eyes.

"Come to big sister, Booboo."

Melody lets him under her blanket, and Martin curls into her embrace. She pats his shoulder to comfort him.

"You had a bad dream?"

Martin nods his head. He is sucking his thumb.

"What did you dream about?"

He shrugs.

"What did you dream about? Did you forget already?"

He nods.

"How can you forget if you're still scared of it?"

He shrugs, then asks, "Dreams can be real?"

"No, dreams are dreams. They cannot come real. This is real." And she points to the things around her room. "Dis is all real. Yo' dreams are yo' dreams. Das all. What did you dream about?"

He shrugs. "I forget."

"Did you dream about the big monster by the waterfall again?"

He nods his head. "Yeh."

"And did the monster chase you again?"

He nods. "And dah monster said he was going eat me alive. He said he wen eat Mama and Daddy and now he going eat me. Dreams can come real?"

"No. No such thing as monsters, Booboo. Das only yo' imagination."

"Whas 'imi-jay-shun'?"

"Das means you only making it up. Like when we make pretend. Dah stuff not real. We only make it up."

"But how come dah monster always talking to me? He no go away. He live by dah waterfall. He stay there."

"What waterfall you talking about? See. You only making dis thing up. You nevah went to the waterfall, right? Right? See. All in yo' imagination."

"Imi-jay-shun."

"Booboo Boy, you silly sometimes."

"He told me I keep running away but he going get me anyway."

"Booboo, I tol' you das only yo' imagination. You made dah dream up. And that means you can change dah dream too. You can tell dah monster whatever you like. You can make him go away if you like."

"Can?"

"Yes, can. You can change the dream. You can wipe out the dream, if you like."

"Can make the dream come real?"

"How can you deny it?" he said.

She pretended not to be listening but engrossed in the activities outside: the men tearing apart the pig's carcass, their voices brash and urgent, working together in syncopation; the women scurrying to catch the dripping fragments of flesh in metal bowls and trays. Sang regarded them, too, sighed, then turned his eyes back to Melody, focusing on the streaks of gray hair that only today he has noticed.

"Melody, don't call your brother a monster. It was you who helped him with his dreams, right? Aren't you just as much to blame for his being the way he was as your cousin Ronnie?"

"How dare you say this to me!" Melody's full anger channeled into his eyes. His brow tightened. Her face had narrowed. She had lost some weight in a matter of minutes.

"How dare you say this to me—and in my own house! In my own house! Sang, if you have nothing else to say, why don't you just get the hell out of here!"

Sang considered the suggestion. He straightened up, took a deep breath, looked outside at the people working over the smoking remains of the pig. Ronnie was peeling off a shard of skin from the chicken wire. The aroma was making Sang hungry for a piece of kalua pig. His mouth salivated.

"If you want me to leave, then I will." His eyes stayed on one of Martin's uncles eating the flesh from a large rib bone.

"Dah way you eat, Uncle Simeon, so 'ono. Man, dah bone stay clean!"

Laughter. A large lusty smile.

"'Ono. Why . . . you jealous?" More laughter. "Here . . . you like one rib bone?"

"Nah-nah. Jus' kidding."

"Eat."

"Nah."

Uncle Simeon waves Ronnie towards him, grabs another rib bone. There's more meat on this one. Uncle Simeon gives the rib a longing look, then offers Ronnie the bone that he has just finished. Laughter. He gives Ronnie the meaty one. Ronnie takes it.

"Eh, Uncle Simeon, thanks, eh."

"No mention."

"I guess I'll leave," Sang said. He waited for a response from Melody, but there was none. The sounds of the party outside now filled the living room.

"They're enjoying themselves, aren't they?" Melody said finally.

"Huh?"

"Those people out there. They're having fun, being with one another. Those hypocrites."

Sang regarded the scene. "Fun? Hypocrites? What do you mean? They're your family out there."

"You see, Sang, there are people who are warm and embracing. And then there are some who are warm and embracing but asses at the same time. Of course, there are those who are purely warm and embracing. But the dangerous ones are those who are at the same time two-faced vampires. The last category includes my brother."

"I never thought I'd hear you say this about your kid brother. You love him. You adored him . . . a lot. Everything he did was wonderful. You used to tell me about his achievements endlessly. That was the gist of most of your conversations with me. It was never about yourself, or . . . about us. It was always about Martin. Martin this and Martin that. And now I hear you cursing your brother, who's dead, and at his memorial dinner. What gives, Melody? What gives?"

As she slowly turns to him, her eyes darken and her smile changes from softness to rigidity, from knowing to disease.

"When a monster is a monster, you don't make excuses for it. If you do, then you become one yourself."

Sang thinks he sees a spot of saliva forming and sparkling at the corner of her mouth. But now he sees a snow-covered mountain spire and then the rush of breaking waves crashing on the shore, thick foam spreading over the sand then returning to the undercurrents for more dispersals and retreats, and more.

The weed from Big Island had taken him beyond the horizon and stars. For Ronnie, the susurrations of water on sand became whisperings between angels and birds. But when the birds began to attack the angels with their beaks, he freaked out. He turned to Martin who, like himself, was stretched out on the dry cool sand on the upside of Kalona Beach.

"Eh, you buzzing?" he said, trembling.

Martin grunted softly from his chest.

Ronnie needed to force a few more words out, to check back into the now. "Dah stuff . . . stay come . . . from Kona. . . . My friend . . . he wen geev me . . . one good deal. . . . Good . . . eh?"

Again, a grunt from Martin.

"So . . . whas it like ovah deah?"

No answer from Martin. He did not notice Martin shake his head. He forced himself to think about something good— sex—to bring himself down from what was turning into a bad trip.

Yeah. The time when I brought the haole girl here from

Sam's party. We got so high in the lifeguard tower, then fucked. Nice big nipples. First time did it with the girl on top of me. What a trip. After the first time, we 'au'au in the ocean, doing it again in the water. What a trip. And then did it again on the beach with the waves breaking on us. Came but out of juice, my balls all squeezed like prunes. Wish she was here right now. I'd be fucking like crazy.

Martin made a gurgling sound.

"Heh? What you said?"

Ronnie waited for an answer. A long time passed. A full moon now had come out of the clouds, and the sand looked like snow.

J'like how was when we was swimming. J'like.

Ronnie grabs his erection and rubs the sweet spot.

Then Martin blurts out: "I doing all this for my family and country. For God and country. God and country. No make sense."

"What? What you said? What no make sense?" He stops rubbing.

"All of this."

"What you talking, Boo?"

"I dunno. I talking about what all of this is about. I play football. I love play football. I got good grades in high school. Everything working out right. Then I go away for college. Football scholarship and everything. The entire free ride. But that's it."

"Whas *that's it?* Eh Boo, you talking haole. Talk local."

"I talking haole? Then let it be. That be it. It be that. Let be that it. Be that it."

Ronnie laughs nervously.

"Eh cuz, you freaking me out. Dis fucking weed cranking you up, eh? Must be dah Kona dirt. How you figgah?"

"I figuring all right. I guess."

"Cuz, no make me laugh."

"I not."

Ronnie watches the moon and the moon turns a rosy color. Which frightens him.

"Eh Boo, what happened to that haole chick you wen score, dah one wit' dah big tits, dah one you showed me dah picture wit' her balancing one can beer on one tit? Eh she was right on, eh? Where was dat?"

"Georgia. Her name was Roberta. Roberta Guernsey. Yeah, she *was*."

"Eh, should've gone visit you. You fucking guy, you had all dah chicks you wanted. I don't mind telling you but I was kinda jealous high school time, you wit' all yo' girlfriends."

"High school *was* high school. Now is now. For God and country. What is this?"

"Eh, there you go again, talking yo' haole."

"Not talking haole, cuz, talking 'the condition.'"

"Cuz, I no understand you. What condition you talking about?"

"You know, a few miles from the college I was going, there's this beautiful waterfall. One night one bunch of us guys on the football team, three of us actually, went there after we got drunk in the dorm. We brought one case beer, and we got these three chicks come with us. We had to park our car in this parking lot, then went over the railing and climbed down this hill. Was really dark and we had to make our way through all these bushes. Then we had to climb up this rocky cliff. Wasn't really a cliff, maybe more like one hill. But was one long, steep climb. And was dark, and I was carrying one case beer and this chick in front of me kept on falling and I had to

catch her and push her up. Finally we got to the top of the hill
which overlooked this lake on the other side, and this is
where you could hear and see the waterfall. It was about one
hundred feet drop.

"It was a real nice night. The stars was all out. There was
no moon, but you still could see the waterfall, the white water
falling and the sound of the rushing water and the mist blowing over you. My friends was having a blast. They was talking
and laughing, and I remember somebody suggesting—but he
was only joking—that we all strip naked and jump down into
the lake. But he was joking. There was a lot of laughter and
giggling. Then somebody started passing around couple joints.
I think one of those chicks wen bring 'em. And we started getting so high, smoking and drinking. I was having a good time,
drinking and getting stoned and getting to know this chick I
was with. But then, all of a sudden, this fricking funny feeling wen come over me.

"I got real cold all of a sudden, real cold. Actually, it was
kinda cold, but the beer made us all warm. But I started shiver-
ing. I tried to keep it from being noticed 'cause everybody was
having such a good time. And then I had this—this—this scary
feeling, like this force was trying pull me over the rocky hill
and yank me hundred feet down to the bottom to the rocks.
I was so scared. The force was tugging at me. I started looking at the stars and it made it even worse cause my mind started
twisting and turning and wondering and wondering all over
the fricken place. I felt like I was being taken to the stars. I
grabbed whatever I could grab on the ground to anchor me
down, the rocks, the dirt. Was clawing into the dirt. I was so
scared this force was going yank me into the darkness of the
bottom of the fall. I don't remember hearing my friends' laugh-

ter anymore. To me everything was silent, everything was con-
spiring to take me down. Cuz, I never had felt that feeling
before. I was so scared, so scared I couldn't think of anything.
But then one strange thing happened.

"I felt the force was inside me, not outside me pulling. It
was inside and trying fo' push me over the cliff. Yeah, it was
inside me, trying fo' push me over. It was telling me fo' run
off the cliff. Run off the cliff, it was telling me. It was *me*, telling
myself to jump. Cuz, *that* was the most scariest feeling I ever
had.

"Man, I held on this piece of rock I was sitting on so hard.
I was so scared. I thought I was going jump up and run off the
cliff. I was so scared.

"Then I started to feel the hill moving, like there was one
earthquake. I was freaking out. I looked at my friends and they
was laughing and partying like nothing was happening. I was
freaking out. I remember saying to myself, 'Shit! What's happening?' And then I realized that the girl I was with was nudging me, trying to pass me one roach, and she was holding back
the cough that the smoke was doing to her. Then she said,
'What did you say? Here, take it. It's good shit, isn't it?'

"My lips was numb, and I wiped them 'cause I thought saliva
was dripping. 'Yeah,' I said. 'The shit's good.' And I took it from
her and took a toke. And somehow that toke warmed me,
calmed me down. And then I passed it back to her and when
she passed it back to the others, I grabbed her and started feeling her up and she started feeling me, and we was in one tangle for one long time. I wanted fo' fuck her so badly. I jus'
wanted fo' fuck her so I wouldn't think about what I was thinking about. But finally she had to stop me 'cause I was trying
to take her jeans off and she didn't want to do it in front of
the others."

They're silent. The only sounds are waves washing over the sand.

"Where do we go from here?" Sang asked.

Melody pulled the photo album towards her. She flipped over the pages of the album indifferently. "I don't know," she said. She stopped at a picture.

"I don't know why I'm going to tell this to you, but—"

"Then don't tell me."

Sang watched Melody's eyes hover over a picture of her parents' wedding.

"It was nice and simple back then," Sang said.

"What was?"

"The weddings, back then. Simple. Two people just fell in love and married. None of these . . . mind games."

"My parents didn't love each other. It was an arrangement. You know that."

"No, I didn't."

"Well, I'm telling you now."

"Then why are you so interested in looking over old pictures of an *unhappy* marriage?"

"Oh, they were happy, but not with each other."

"So why not enjoy this party? Why not enjoy what you already have? Why *look at old pictures?*"

"Because," she said, looking out the doorway and then at Sang, "I'm creating my own family history. A history of what should not have happened and . . . what should have." She tossed her hair back as if to shake off an impediment. "I'm going to make sure that this history comes to life."

"What do you mean you're changing your family's history? If something already happened, how can you stop it from already happening?"

They all think him he such one saint. Uh-uh. No ways one saint. One sinner. Nobody knew him dah way I knew him. Heh. Everybody think he was such one All-American. Ain't no way going fool me. I was there wit' him and saw him fo' what he really was. Dah fuckah was one freak. One fucking freak. If anybody was one blame fo' him being dis way was 'cause hes own maddah and hes crybaby sistah, Mele. Dey made him something out of nothing. I know. I seen him fo' what he was. Nothing mo', nothing less. Dah fuckah was one thief, one addict, one con artist. And I tell you dis: Everybody think he was one lady's man. Nah, no ways. He used to pay fo' get one fuck. And how many wahines he wen raped. He wasn't no lady's man. No ways. Eh I wen get mo' cunt den him, many mo'. I give you one example fo' illustrate my point.

One afternoon we went cruising down Sandy's, having a few brews. We parked next to dis haole chick sitting all alone by herself in her car checking the surf. Not bad chick. I was in the driver's seat and I tol' her, "Eh girl, you like taste some good weed?" And she was all smiles. Think she was smoking already cause her eyes were all fucked up. So she got out of her car, she wen fall down but she made it to my back seat, and I lit dis winner stuff I got from dah Big Island. Shit, two tokes and you gone. So we was smoking dis stuff, and me and dis chick was jamming, talking all kinds. Martin was out of it. He was jus' looking out at dah waves, if he was looking. He was quiet, he was like dat dah whole day since I wen pick him up from his house. I think he jus' wen come back from college fo' dah summer. Dah fuckah always had dah breaks. Anyways, I swung around, started rapping to dah chick. I put my arm in back and then I started stroking her knee, then her thigh. Eh, she was getting off of dat. Her eyes was closing. And den Boo, dat fucking Boo . . .

There is nothing to see outside, except low-hanging, gray clouds. A promise of sun, perhaps, but that quickly fades.

She hears the rustling of coconut fronds. Cars whizzing by frequently, having gotten off the rush-hour freeway, going home. Below, seven floors down, children playing. She loosens the damp towel to expose her other breast, cups both breasts with her hands. The touch is cold, but she feels a warmth growing inside. The breasts are full, perhaps not as full as they should be, or could be. But enough to please any man? She rubs the nipples and feels a strong current spreading from her center. She stops. Is this wrong?

At times like this, she yearns for the feeling she has desired for a long time. She does not know how it feels, only yearns to experience it. Some of the mothers who come to the classroom doorway to pick up their children seem eternally carrying burdens of proof, waddling around helplessly, some with pubescent faces breaking out with pimples, holding another child in hand, perhaps a future student of hers. Most of these mothers seem barely out of high school, perhaps some barely out of intermediate school, if they did go to school. Speaking the language of the uneducated, watching television all day long, eating crackers and chips and chocolates, and drinking chilled Cokes by the carton. Are they happy doing what they're doing? Don't they aspire to something higher in life? Is this their fate, to be bearers of flesh for their husbands, boyfriends, lovers?

She unravels the towel further, lets it spread apart over her stomach and fall to the sides, exposing herself completely to the gray still air, the gray cold air of dusk. She folds her legs to her chest and, closing her eyes, runs her fingers down to meet in those thick folds of flesh and pubic hair. And here she slips fingertips into that oozing moisture, then works her way up to the tip of a sprouting sensation.

She stops, withdraws her hand, opens her eyes.

There are eyes watching.

Suddenly she feels naked. And shamed.

She covers herself and cowers. Her eyes cross the room and glower for a moment on the bronze crucifix affixed to the wall behind the television. Lowering her eyes, she hurries to the bathroom to slip on something warm.

"You're not listening to me, Sang! You always don't listen to me!"

"What exactly are you trying to say?"

"You don't know? *You just don't know?* Sang!"

"Tell me, I'm listening."

"I've been telling you for all these years, seventeen to be exact. And you *still* don't get it. You still don't get it!"

"Tell me!"

"No!"

"Why?"

"Because it's useless. It's—"

Mama Rapoza approaches the screen door, her face shadowed as she presses it against the screen, squinting her eyes. "Whas dah commotion? Melody, what you talkin' about? Who you talking to?"

"It's all right, Mama."

"Who's dat? Sang? Sang, why you no come us'side?"

"Later, Mama." Wasn't she wearing someting else? Another color?

"Sang, I'm glad you came. And wheah yo' maddah? She nevah come?"

"No. She feeling sick."

"Das right. You tol' me dat already. But what you guys talkin' about? You guys fightin'? What you guys talkin' about?"

"Nothing, Ma."

"Nothin' no sound like nothin'."

"It's nothing, Ma."

"Den why you guys yellin'? Can hear all ovah dah creation? Sang, what you guys talkin' about?"

Sang regards Melody's lowering, dimming face, the graying hairs at her temples. And the sparkling diamond earring that he now notices behind a wisp of dark hair.

She never wears earrings. Never.

"History, Mama," Sang says. "We're talking about history."

The phone rings.

"Hello?"

"Mele? Is dis you?"

A pause. "Yeah, Ma."

"Mele, are you sick? How come you not going work? I . . . getting worried about you. Yo' work place call me and ask me why you not coming work."

"Who called you? The school? The principal?"

"I dunno. Was one man's voice."

"Brian."

"Who's dat?"

"Never mind. The principal."

"Mele, what's dah matter wit' you? You in some kinda trouble?"

"No, Ma. I just . . . haven't been feeling too well lately. But I'm getting over it."

"You get dah flu?"

"No. Nothing like that. I just . . . been a bit tired."

"You want me come over and make you some soup?"

"No. It's okay. I'm all right now. I'm going back to work tomorrow."

"Tomorrow?"

"Yes. Don't worry, Mama. It's . . . just a mild cold. That's what it is."

"One cold? You sure you no want me come over and make you some bean soup?"

"No, Mama. I'll be all right. I'll be all right."

She says goodbye and returns the receiver to its cradle. She is feeling tired. It was a wonderfully long night, last night. She stretches her arms toward the ceiling and yawns. She needs to go . . . back. Again.

Drifting to the still warm bed. Slipping under the rippling covers. Writhing and stretching her limbs with the luxury of softness.

A hand searches for the folds of flesh and hair moistened still from the early morning meeting, then fingers the hardening tip of her desire.

Where were you? Where did you go?

She closes her eyes and merges with the voice in her mind. Where is he? There . . . there he is. There . . . you are.

From a cool mist, a dark hard form emerges. Muscular arms reach out. The face is blurred, but she knows it is him. Yes. And he reaches out and embraces her, his tongue searching for hers, his hands roaming before, above, behind, below and between. And again she's coming towards a dawning of the senses.

"Well I hope you folks are having a good time."

"Yes, Ma." Melody's eyes pried at Sang's colorless face: *Why don't you say something?* "We're all right, Ma."

"Sang, did you get anything to eat?"

"No, Mama."

"Then come out here and help yo'self. You know you can jus' help yo'self here, right? Dis is like yo' own home."

"Yes, Mama. Thank you."

Mama returned to the pig. Sang's eyes followed her to the picnic table on which metal pans of smoking meat were placed.

"Sang, I have something to say to you."

"What is it?" His eyes were still watching Mama.

"Sang, I don't know how to say this to you, but I'm . . . I'm with a child."

Silence. Laughing outside.

"So," Sang began, coolly, "do you want to get married?"

"The child is not yours."

"Yes, I know. Do you want to get married?"

"Don't you want to know whose child it is?"

"Do you want to get married?"

"Did you hear what I said? The child is not yours."

"Yes, I heard that. But I'm asking you, do you want to get married."

"No . . . not to you."

Sang severed his eyes from the celebration outside. "Will you marry the child's father, then?"

"No." Melody took in a long breath, releasing it with difficulty. "I'm not getting married. The child has no father."

She hangs up the receiver. She wishes the phone wouldn't ring so often. Disturbing her sleep.

Why don't they just leave me alone?

Her face falls shaking into a cradle of trembling hands. A dull pain stabs the left side of her body. She straightens up, cringes, and follows with the palm of her hand the pain meandering across the soft dome of her abdomen. Then the pain disappears, as if plucked off by a magic finger of air. She runs her fingers through her tangled mess of hair, drawing the ends together in the back.

No. I've got to get back on my feet. I've got to go back to work. This is killing me.

She drags herself back to the bedroom, then turns instead into the bathroom where she pauses in front of the mirror just enough to see what a wreck she has become: hair like flowing flames of black fire; redden, swollen eyes; face puffed and marked with lines of sleep.

How can I return to work? I look so . . . terrible.

She backs away, eyes fallen, and lumbers to the bed where she lies on her side, on sheets undone at the corners, adjusts breasts that have enlarged and become sensitive to touch. (The changes of her body have been accompanied by an appetite for Kona Coffee ice cream, canned sardines in oil, and oranges, cravings she has never known.) She turns on her back. Her eyes focus in and out at the gray spackled ceiling. She commands herself to get up and take a cold shower, to wake up out of a gloom that she has been in for the past three or four days— she can't remember how long—but her limbs do not move, they are weighed by a warm, sticky mist now entering her mind. The dark form appears, groping through the thickness. The face emerges, one that she is too familiar with, and fears.

No, you mustn't! This is not right! THIS IS NOT RIGHT!

But the face smiles in conquest—he has her—and his hard body rubs against her, and his strong hands rove all over her body, massages and soothes the tightening in her bosom. He laughs soundlessly, playfully, his eyes squinting and sparkling, as if saying *But that is why it is right!* She pushes him away, but he snatches her weak flailing arms and pins her, and she struggles but weakens and finally succumbs to the probing licks of his tongue. He enters and she releases and accepts.

It is happening again. She cannot resist anymore. She cannot stop his thrusts, each one empowering her with sensations that are breaking her body, that vibrate to the ends of her body, that forces her to withdraw further and further from resistance, that are melded into a madly churning, compressed bulb of pleasure and resentment.

"I think Booboo needs one beeg hug."

He is crying again. From another nightmare of the water monster chasing him. What does this monster look like? Why does he have these dreams? Will he outgrow them? Oh, Booboo. Come to Sister Big.

"Booboo, what's the matter? You had another nightmare?"

Martin nods his head. Wipes the tears from his eyes. Then slips under the covers and latches on to Melody. Hugging her tightly.

"Booboo, it's only a dream, okay? Only a dream. Is not real."

"Is."

"No, it's not. Listen to your Sister Big."

"But dah stuff always chasing me. Everywhere I go."

"What does the monster look like? Is it Daddy?"

Booboo is silent. "Dah monster stay chasing me."

"But das only one dream. Only in your dream it going to chase you. Das all."

"No. Dah stuff stay chasing me everyday kine. Honest."

"No-no, Booboo. Only in your dream it stay chasing you."

"Not."

The "not" is weak, swallowed before the full word is heard.

"You going listen to me or you going let the monster catch you?"

He's silent. He hugs his older sister, tucks his head under her chin.

"I love you, Mele."

Melody hugs him back. "And me, you."

"Mele, chase dah monster away. Bus' him up fo' me, Mele. Geev him dirty lickings, Mele. Push him away."

"I going. Jus' keep hugging me and dah monster going run away."

He going run away. Run away. Run away.

She bends over the bathroom basin, supported by her elbows, heaves and heaves and spits out the bile of mistrust.

It's the third time in here this morning, and the nausea isn't getting better. Yet she cannot refuse the oily saltiness of sardines and the thick sweetness of ice cream that are stocked in the refrigerator. A half hour later she's back in the bathroom, her rib cage contracting painfully, the stomach convulsing and ejecting the smelly curds of her folly, the smell further nauseating her, until nothing but burning liquid dribbles from her lips numbed by the bad taste. It is an awful feeling to be married to the bathroom sink, watching a liquid life ooze down the drain. She rinses her mouth several times, unable to rid herself completely of the bad taste, then brushes her teeth and gargles with a strong antiseptic mouthwash and returns to the bedroom, collapsing again on the bed.

Her head swirls, her eyes unable to follow the dizzying vortex of her mind, her eyes unable to stay open. But the inner eyes are worse: She is falling down a dark abyss. She opens her eyes, spreads her arms as if to stabilize the body's contortious falling. It steadies little, the bed revolving on a wobbly axis.

Outside a mejiro sings, then another in a nearby tree. The phone rings. She lets it ring. *Let it ring.* She counts the rings:

one, two, three . . . seven. The room lightens with the sun blooming out of the clouds. Suddenly she has the urge to grab her ring of keys and throw it at the birds.

She has my eyes, this baby of mine. My warm brown eyes that have seen the mainland and home, home only after mainland. She is pretty, momona like her mother was when she was a baby, like in that picture on the piano in Ma's living room. Boy, do I miss smelling that house. That homey smell. But cannot help. What's done is done. No can do nothing about it already. Can just hope for the best, for everybody, especially for pure joy here, ku'uipo o ka lani. Her mama is real gentle with her. They look so nice lying there sleeping together. Baby's eyes closed and mouth a teeny bit open, her mama cradling her and sleeping at the same time. She has gone through a crazy time, I know. But what's got to be done, has to be done. I wish I could touch their hair and warm skin, feel their sweet breathing together, smell the smells of this motherhood and child. But I must be content with what I have. It will fade away, I know, but at least for these delicious moments I can come to know this air, this air of what I am. I must remember this hope before it vanishes, forever. And ever.

That's the beauty of words: to run, to record. *That's the beauty of dreams:* to remember, to construct. *That's the beauty of lovers:* to mend, to trust.

So said Martin as he floated above in the sky of the cloudless room, looking down and over and through and under the love of his life, his daughter of three-weeks-and-mere-hours, that laughter and murmuring of love that he so maddeningly wishes he can touch, that little pudding cuddled next to mother/wife/sister, sister of those waning years of life that he seemed not to have held in hand, those years gossamer like heavy warm sticky vapor, like thick translucent water flopping through fingers. So much love, a love supreme, so indescribably untouchable, *même choses*: how can a baby be so beautiful, so pure—an essence unseen—and so full of random attachments? how can? how how? and where to now? must I regret what has happened? what will happen? why can't I cry and weep, tears releasing me to wind and while the clouds roar above me, around me, these clouds that flow through me and know my mind? I don't want to be these clouds—no! *Never!* but they are already talking to me as if I am theirs owned. *No!* blinding my senses! I need my touch! *Keep away!*

LIBRARY OF CONGRESS CATALOGING-
IN-PUBLICATION DATA

Pak, Gary, 1952–
Language of the geckos and other stories / Gary Pak.
p. cm.—(The Scott and Laurie Oki series
in Asian American studies)
ISBN 0-295-98527-5 (pbk. : alk. paper)
1. Hawaii—Social life and customs—Fiction.
2. Asian Americans—Fiction.
I. Title. II. Series.
PS3566.A39L36 2005
813'.54—dc22   2005007880

ACKNOWLEDGMENTS

"Hae Soon's Song" originally appeared in *Literary
Realm* (1991); *The Best of Honolulu Fiction: Stories
from the Honolulu Magazine Fiction Contest*, ed.
Eric Chock and Darrell Lum (Honolulu: Bamboo
Ridge Press, 1999); *Crossing Into America: The New
Immigrants and Their Experience since 1965*, ed. Louis
Mendoza and S. Shankar (New York: The New Press,
2003); and *Yobo: Korean American Writing in Hawai'i*
(Honolulu: Bamboo Ridge Press, 2003). "My Friend
Kammy" originally appeared in *Hawai'i Review* 24
(Fall 1988): 61–73. "A House of Mirrors" originally
appeared in *Hawai'i Review* 32 (Spring 1991): 129–40.
"Rebirth" originally appeared in *Century of the Tiger:
One Hundred Years of Korean Culture in America,
1903–2003*, ed. Jenny Ryun Foster, Frank Stewart,
and Heinz Insu Fenkl (Honolulu: *Manoa*,
University of Hawai'i Press, 2003).